Praise for
Lima Nights

"Tightly written, page-turning prose . . . [Marie Arana] is masterful in telling this unsentimental story of obsession."
—*San Antonio Express-News*

"[*Lima Nights*] has a deliberate simplicity and lucidity that allows the reader to peer far beneath the surface of Peruvian culture. . . . The final outcome is a true, cinematic cliffhanger that seems both poignant and right."
—*San Francisco Chronicle*

"An erotic, catastrophic love story that grows more mysterious by the page, Arana's novel of taboo passion, tragic misperception, and life's hidden dimensions is as shattering as it is seductive."
—*Booklist*

"[A] quite grown-up story of love across class and ethnic lines in South America, where such things do not go unnoticed. . . . Brooding and elegant."
—*Kirkus Reviews*

"An unflinching look at a troubled relationship . . . Highly recommended."
—*Library Journal*

"Soars with poetic imagery, evocative description and moving characterization."
—*Rocky Mountain News*

Lima Nights

A NOVEL

MARIE ARANA

DIAL PRESS TRADE PAPERBACKS

ACKNOWLEDGMENTS

I am deeply indebted to my brilliant editor, Susan Kamil, whose faith in me gives me courage. My agent, Amanda Urban, is my lucky star. I am more grateful than I can say to my father's childhood friend Pablo Schmidt for long conversations about German Peruvians; to my godmother Isabel Arana Cisneros for finding old records of the Club Germania; and to Monica Klien, whose lists of German immigrants to Peru were invaluable. A deep bow to Mercedes Chavez Quiroz, who spirited me away more than once to give me a glimpse into the extraordinary world of *videntes*. Thanks, too, to my patient husband, Jonathan Yardley, who read many drafts of this novel and never failed to encourage me. Of course, I alone am responsible for its flaws.

2010 Dial Press Trade Paperback Edition

Published in the United States by Dial Press Trade Paperbacks, an imprint of The Random House Publishing Group, a division of Random House, Inc., New York.

DIAL PRESS and DIAL PRESS TRADE PAPERBACKS are registered trademarks of Random House, Inc., and the colophon is a trademark of Random House, Inc.

Originally published in hardcover in the United States by The Dial Press, an imprint of The Random House Publishing Group, a division of Random House, Inc., in 2009.

Library of Congress Cataloging-in-Publication Data
Arana, Marie
Lima nights / Marie Arana.
p. cm.
ISBN: 978-0-385-34259-9
1. Lima (Peru)—Fiction. I. Title.

PS3601.R345 L56 2009   2008032357
813/.6 22

Printed in the United States of America
www.dialpress.com

9 8 7 6 5 4 3 2 1

Book design by Helene Berinsky

For Lalo and Adam

I don't love her anymore, that's for sure, but maybe I love her.
So brief is the love, so long the forgetting.

Ya no la quiero, es cierto, pero tal vez la quiero.
Es tan corto el amor, y es tan largo el olvido.

—PABLO NERUDA

Part One

CARLOS AND MARIA

SPRING 1986

• • •

Lima nights! And a pretty dancer!
What more could you ask for, friend?
—Poster from a dance bar
Lima, Peru

1

Carlos

"GIVE ME YOUR HAND."

It was dark in the bar, the air thick with cigarette smoke and the salt stink of pisco and perspiration, but he could see that she was as lovely as she had seemed from across the room. She was standing with one hand outstretched. Her hair was long, black, heavy; her teeth white and straight behind the radiant smile.

"Come. You've been staring at me long enough. You want to dance?"

He felt the fever of the evening's accumulated drink make a slow, pleasant course for his brain. His friends were laughing, slapping the hard oak with their hands. Someone shouted, "Bluhm! She wants to see you move! Go on! Give her something to look at!"

They had come from the Club Germania, the venerable establishment on the outskirts of the capital where they had spent a quiet evening with their wives, who plied them with pork chops and applesauce, goulash and spaetzle. Escorting the four happy matrons to Oscar's sleek black Mercedes, they had instructed his chauffeur to take them to a nearby parlor for ice cream. The men would go off to Las Americas for brandy and cigars.

But it wasn't to Las Americas that they had gone. Willy, who had long been carrying on with a woman in San Borja, had a better idea. There was a place not far from Carmela's apartment, he told them—Noches Lindas. Good bolero, fresh Havanas, pretty women.

Willy being Willy, his description was wrong on most counts: It was tango, not bolero. The cigars were stale. The sign over the door read Noches Limeñas—Lima Nights. But the women were reasonably good looking, the only exception a toothy mestiza with orange hair.

They had taken a table a good distance from the dance floor so that they could survey the lot. Clearly, some of the women had come with men—or would be leaving with them. They were draped over the men's shoulders, stroking their hair, nuzzling their necks. The ones with red collars were employees of the bar, the waiter explained, and available as dance partners. All you had to do was wiggle a finger.

Marco, a genial hotel manager and ever the catalyst where women were concerned, had been the first to call one over. She was delicate as a bird—tiny and freckled—pale for a Negro, hair bleached the color of wheat. "Why her?" Willy barked, as she made her way to their table.

"Why do you think?" Marco barked back over the loud music. "She looks German! A bit more nose, a bit less lip, and she could be my cousin Hilda."

They laughed and watched him go off, the three of them content to sit and take in the liquor.

It was true Bluhm had been ogling the one with long dark hair. There was, after all, the matter of her dress—black, with red straps and a rippling red frill along the hem. Slit to one hip, it clung to her, so that there was no mystery about the curve of her breasts or the sweet little shape of her ass. It was the dress that got his attention. Then came the rest: The nut-brown skin, smooth, dusted here and there with gold glitter. The angel face, the scarlet pout of her lips. And, finally, the red velvet ribbon that circled her neck, signaling her status as an available partner.

The loud, fluttering wail of the bandoneón drowned out the men's voices, but he no longer cared what they were saying. With an impish grin, Bluhm beckoned the woman closer. She leaned in. "I don't do the tango," he said.

"Sure you do," she countered, her voice resolute and deep. "You just haven't tried. And no one has taught you."

He could smell her perfume at that distance: brisk, clean, tart as fruit. Was it apple? Quince? He couldn't tell. But fruit it emphatically was, the kind of fragrance his wife had never favored, preferring as she did the subtle, warm scent of tuberoses. Earlier that evening, kissing their sons good night, Sophie had swept a silk scarf over her shoulders and filled the room with the redolence of those diminutive white flowers. Even out in the vestibule he'd noted it. It was an aptitude he'd always had—that strong, indisputable sense of smell. Totally useless for an importer of cameras.

"Go on, Carlos!" His friends were pounding the table with fists now. "Don't disappoint the lady!" Lady. They knew all too well he had an appetite for *cholas*—the browner the better. But he wouldn't have called any one of his conquests a lady.

Maybe it was the scent of their skin—the sharp bouquet of it, as natural and welcoming as loam. Or the small hands and feet. The perfect hairlessness of their bodies. The cunning tilt of their eyes. All of it so different from, so antithetical to Bluhm, whose hands were large, skin like milk, eyes blue. Or Bluhm's wife, for that matter.

In all his forty-four years, he had never known anyone who looked less Peruvian than Sophie. She, like Bluhm, had been raised entirely in Spanish, on Creole food, in the heart of the Inca continent. But, like him, she was fair and blond, a real Teuton. The years had been kind to Sophie—she still had her slender figure, hair the color of a German autumn—but time had sharpened her features, hardened her jaw. Since the birth of Rudy sixteen years ago, her lips, which always had been daintily bowed, had settled into a grim line. Eventually, a certain severity—a Berliner elegance, his mother called it—had taken command of her face.

He stood and let the woman lead him to the floor. She was smiling over one shoulder, tossing her black mane with all the vigor of an eager pony. There was something exhilarating about her. Wild. The bandoneón was at full throttle now, and the player was pumping his long arms, sending quick fingers across the buttons. A fat man in an ill-fitting suit crooned, "*Te ha-a-a entrado muy adentro en el pobre cora-a-azón!*"

The *chola* took his hands and began a simple two-step, as if she were teaching a slow child. It was easy to follow. In the distance, he could see Marco twirling the yellow-haired Negress under one arm. Bluhm couldn't help but laugh, and his partner laughed with him. She placed Bluhm's right hand firmly against the small of her back and held it there as she looked up triumphantly. "See?" she said. "This is the tango. You've mastered the first lesson."

They finished the dance and he and his friends left shortly afterward. He thought little more of the woman in the tight black dress until he was taking off his clothes in the dark of his bedroom. Reaching into a pocket to fish out his keys, he felt an unfamiliar bit of paper, no larger than a business card. By the light of the bathroom, he read:

> Juana Maria Fernandez
> For Your Next Lesson, call: 466-0777.

THE NEXT TIME he saw her was at Santa Isabel, the fancy new Chilean-owned supermarket on the Avenida Camino Real. He was with his son, wheeling along a cart filled with ingredients for pilsner, which he liked to make in the comfort of his own kitchen. He turned the corner and there she was, standing to one side of a cash register, moving someone's groceries efficiently off the conveyor belt into bags.

He didn't recognize her immediately, although he was drawn to the face. Her hair was pulled into a tidy knot at the nape of her neck and she wore no lipstick, but, as she chatted with the cashier animatedly, the unmistakable loveliness was there and, when he scoured his memory, he remembered the dress, the fruity perfume, and the drunken night—two weeks before—when a woman with the same face had led him to the dance floor.

"Here, Fritz," he said to his son before he could think better of it, "let's get in line over here."

"Why?" the lanky nineteen-year-old protested. "That register there has fewer people!" Fritz was too tall for his trousers, disheveled, a halo of amber curls framing his face, and he spoke with a young person's certitude that grown-ups were inferior creatures. Seeing his father move in the opposite direction, he sighed and slouched along like an obliging dog.

The woman computed the situation immediately. She had seen Bluhm standing in line, inching his way toward her. By the time the cashier was ready to check him through, she had calculated that the boy was his son, the groceries were for his wife, and, more than likely, the store they were standing in was in easy radius of his neighborhood.

"Good to see you, sir."

The voice was strong and thrilling, full of welcome—hinting at all the ways a woman might please a man. He remembered hearing that voice in the din of the tango bar.

"You work here now?"

She looked up from under her thick eyelashes. "I work here *too*."

Fritz straightened to his full height and looked from his father's face to hers and back again with quick curiosity.

"In both places! Really? And when do you ever sleep?" Bluhm reached casually for his wallet, enjoying the secrets in that very public conversation.

She laughed and pulled the six gallons of distilled water, four packets of yeast, and jar of malt syrup from the aluminum table into plastic bags, working her small hands nimbly. The cashier, deprived now of her sunny attention, punched the register's buttons glumly and kept to himself.

"So, this is your son, señor?"

"Yes. This is Fritz. Come on, Fritz, be polite, say hello to . . . Juana?"

"Maria. I go by my middle name."

"Ah." Then, turning to Fritz, "Maria also works in a restaurant in San Borja. She's waited on me there. She's a *friend*."

Fritz nodded, understanding the clear exaggeration of the word, the grace of it—men of his father's class were not friends to waitresses. He said hello dutifully and, his curiosity satisfied, shuffled off to look at wristwatches on a faraway counter.

Bluhm studied the young woman more closely now, trying to square the demure vision before him with the voluptuous bargirl he had held briefly in his arms. She looked to be in her twenties—round face, a doll's chin, small nose, more jungle than mountain Indian—and, in the full light of day, he could see that her complexion was smooth and perfect, as burnished as marble. But she was something of a paradox too: In the full light of day, she seemed straightforward, guileless—

not at all the sort of woman who would slip her number into a stranger's coat.

"You never came back for your second lesson," she said, pushing the reloaded cart toward him.

"No," he said, and winked at her openly. "But don't give up on me yet, sweetheart. I'm not as slow-footed as I seem."

BLUHM CHATTED IDLY with his son as he pulled the old black car past the open gate into the driveway of 300 Avenida Rivera. He didn't have to step foot inside his house to know that Sophie was at the piano and Rudy in the straight-backed chair at her side. The boy was playing his cello—he was better than good at it—and the sad, plangent strains of Bach's *"Erbarme Dich"* rode out of the house's elaborate windows into the bright November afternoon.

Bluhm motioned for Fritz to carry in the groceries while he sat in the car a few minutes longer, allowing the music to fill his senses. It was a piece his father had played on that same cello every Sunday, after the siesta—a poignant prayer set to music. Every weekend of Bluhm's childhood, for as long as he could remember, he had wakened to that inexpressibly mournful melody, and now here was his younger son, rendering it beautifully, echoing a past he had never known.

Bluhm closed his eyes and breathed in the sweetness of his garden. He could smell the bougainvillea cascading down the wall, the peach trees thrusting their fleecy new progeny into spring, the hosta lilies, like so many soldiers, lining the walk in triumphant welcome. He caught the scent of his mother's lilacs, arching over the double doors and tumbling down along the latticework. She had planted them herself, well before his father had died, well before Bluhm and Sophie had moved in—when 300 Avenida Rivera had hummed with servants and dinners were punctuated by the pop of champagne corks, when German bankers from Stuttgart stood out on the veranda, taking in the night's fragrance and stars.

The house was still grand. No one could deny it. Nestled between the Golf Club and the ancient pyramids, it sat at the very heart of San Isidro—in a neighborhood whose shops sported French names and catered to women with haughty faces. The streets here were clean, hosed down by gardeners every morning; the walls freshly painted every spring. Standing guard in the magnificent doorways of the commercial establishments were armed sentries in handsome uniforms, whose only apparent charge was to shoo off the beggars who stumbled in now and then from the heartbreaking dunghills of Lima.

Bluhm's house stood on as a tribute to the family affluence, even if that affluence was now largely gone. It had stood through the First World War, when Carlos's grandfather Johann Bluhm had been drafted along with hundreds of other Latin Americans of German origin to serve in the kaiser's army. It had stood through the Second, when two Nazi diplomats from the embassy had come around, sat under the house's vaulted ceilings, drunk schnapps, and insisted, to no avail, that Johann's son, Rodolfo, do the right thing and join the Wehrmacht. It had stood on through the boom days of the

'50s, when Rodolfo was made head representative of the Deutsche Bank in Lima; when he and his wife, Dorotea, left little Carlos to roam its vast halls with four nursemaids, a butler, and three cooks, while they toured the world on the *Queen Elizabeth*. It stood on in the early '70s when the socialists parceled out the rural haciendas of the rich to the peons; when Dorotea, by then a widow, shuttered her windows against anyone with a possible eye for the family silver. And it was standing now, in this nervous decade of terrorism, in a country festooned with barbed wire and bedeviled by random violence. It was standing fast, even though Carlos Bluhm was no banker but an ordinary, run-of-the-mill camera salesman— even though the entire nation seemed trapped in a postlapsarian limbo and its unfinished buildings and bridges hung like mastodons in midair, half born, and waiting for issue.

He went in through the massive front door. A vase of mountain lilies was on the foyer table and the light through the stained glass in the ceiling shone down, turning the striated petals into jewels. Nearby, the maid Manuela was sweeping the staircase. She nodded deferentially as Bluhm strode past toward the music.

The moment Rudy saw his father's face at the door, he set aside the cello and ran into his arms. He was smaller, more compact than Fritz, with an easy confidence that was rare for a boy his age. Bluhm pushed him away, mussed his hair, then grabbed his head and thrust it playfully under one arm. Giggling, Rudy butted him onto the ivory sofa, where Bluhm surrendered. Sophie smiled and turned from the piano, smoothing the wrinkles in her skirt.

"Willy called while you were out," she said. "He didn't say why, but he wants you to call back today."

Bluhm raised an eyebrow.

She sighed. "You know how I feel about Willy."

"Yes. Well."

"Honestly, I just don't trust him. Who could? With that love nest of his in San Borja. He's absolutely shameless, and everybody—"

Bluhm waved a cautionary finger and nodded toward their son.

"But Rudy's the one who told me!" she cried. "He was over there, visiting Willy's boys, when Willy and Beatriz started in with one of their screaming matches." Bluhm glanced at his son, who was studying his knees as if he'd just discovered them.

"What he's putting his poor wife through!" she continued. "It's infuriating. And then there's little Pedro—all of twelve! Pedro told Rudy that his parents were fighting about the woman in San Borja. That all they seem to do anymore is yell at each other about that slut."

The word brought him to his feet. "That's none of my business, Sophie. Willy has been my best friend for as long as I can remember. I'm not going to judge him. And I'm certainly not going to ignore his calls."

"All right. But I have to be honest with you, Carlos, and I don't mind saying this in front of Rudy: That 'best friend' of yours is nothing but trouble. I want all my angels perched on my shoulders when he's around. I know you and your friends think he's great company, and in the old days I thought so too.

But we're not children anymore, darling—and what he's doing to Beatriz . . . Well, it disgusts me. He's an arrogant, selfish little man." Sophie rose, whisked the newspaper off the coffee table, and walked briskly toward the staircase.

When Bluhm called Willy back later that afternoon, all Sophie's angels were clearly distracted. This was the point at which all the trouble would begin.

"Willy?"

"Carlos! I've been deputized to organize a little recreation. The boys want to meet Thursday night at the club."

"What for?"

"A glass of pisco. A bowl of peanuts. A bit of mischief. What else?"

"In that stuffy old place? Count me out. But call me back if you change your mind and decide to go someplace more fun."

"Such as?"

"Such as the place you took us to a few weeks ago, *dummkopf.* That tango hole, remember?"

There was a brief silence while Willy thought it over. "If we go there, I can bring Carmela," he said brightly. And so it was agreed.

For the next three days Bluhm busied himself with the usual projects. He sat at the desk in his father's study, which he had fashioned into an office, and made up a tidy list of all he needed to do. There were calls to make. There were clients to attend to: The Hiraoka appliance store wanted to put in a large order for Zeiss lenses, and there was a rumor that the newspaper *El Comercio* would soon be updating its camera equipment. With a heavy black suitcase of samples in hand, he called on the Hiraoka brothers and instructed them on the virtues of the new lenses: the increased power of the zoom, the higher quality of nickel, the multicoated protective filters.

Later that day, he telephoned the photo editor at *El Comercio* and was put on hold, causing his mind to drift off to memories of a receptionist he'd known at that newspaper two or three years before—a woman with shiny black eyes and a wonderful, feral laugh. He had waxed eloquent about that laugh over three or four pisco sours one night before she agreed to sleep with him. They had hurried back to the newspaper, found an empty office, and wrestled each other to the floor in a coupling he later regretted. She called him at home day after day, whining for his attention. When Sophie happened to answer one morning, the woman, in all brazenness, left a message for Bluhm, complete with her name. He'd had to yell at her from a phone booth, threaten to call the police.

The secretary finally came on, forcing him to push the whole miserable business from his mind. Yes, the pert voice said, the editor would see him on Friday. He should come prepared to show his wares.

On Wednesday, after supper, when Rudy had gone off to bed, Bluhm decided to make the pilsner. It was a week before Fritz's final exams at the university and, suspecting the boy needed a healthy distraction, he called him down to the kitchen, where he had already enlisted Manuela to crush the hops. Clattering their way through the cavernous cabinets in the pantry, they got out the necessary bowls, pots, bottles, and ladles and lined them all up on the open counter. Before long, Dorotea, Bluhm's seventy-seven-year-old mother, wandered in, lured by the jolly racket.

Fritz was in especially high spirits that night as he lorded over the great enamel pot, stirring the malt syrup into the boiling hops. He stood at the hot stove, pink-faced, bright-eyed, and presided over the conversation. He was full of tales about how his friends got into trouble with their professors. One who was chronically late to history class had been made to write a paper on the virtues of punctuality. "Paco, of all people!" Fritz bellowed. "Who's late to everything! Who was probably late the day he was born and who'll be late to his own funeral, unless they nail him to the coffin! And that fool's supposed to write about being on time? Ay!" And his grandmother giggled like a girl. It was as pleasant an evening as Bluhm had ever spent with Fritz, and it did his soul good to see that for all the vestiges of an awkward adolescence, the boy had a quick head and blithe heart. Seeing him flushed and smiling, bantering easily with his grandmother, Bluhm imagined what a fine man he might become.

Dorotea, too, had been delightful in her way. She was a determined little woman, radiantly energetic, and that energy shone nowhere so much as in her blue eyes, which had a way of squinting when she listened, rendering them bright points of tourmaline. She fixed these on Fritz now, and Bluhm could see how she relished the boy's exuberance—how free she seemed of her never-ending worry about the boys. It was dangerous, she always claimed, to be young, male, in a country nettled by history, with so much uncertainty ahead.

Dorotea was nothing like Sophie. Bluhm's mother was as hot-tempered and restless as his wife was cool and serene. Dorotea loved to argue; Sophie could only seethe. Dorotea pleaded with her daughter-in-law to be more sociable; Sophie would only demur. But through the years the two had managed to achieve a kind of solidarity. They had lived side by side, settled their differences, won each other's trust, and, over time, their mutual respect had turned into something like love.

He had met Sophie at one of those stifling cotillions at the Club Germania, arranged, like tribal rituals, to encourage marriage between young people of German descent. His father had pointed her out, charmed by her delicate features and porcelain white shoulders. She had been eighteen at the time, a fragile flower but rooted in all the gentle graces. Musical, cultured, polite, she excelled in the trait his father considered most pleasing in a woman: unwavering civility. "Those other frauleins look like good fun," his father told him the next day at dinner, "but Sophie Westermann is the very picture of perfection. If I were you, I'd go after her, boy!" Bluhm took his father's suggestion and began calling on her. By the time Sophie was twenty, they were married, though Dorotea was, at best, only tolerant of the union, preferring a more spirited breed of woman for her son. But when Fritz was born, Bluhm's mother softened. She noted the passion behind Sophie's reserve: the doting attention to the baby, the gift for mothering no one had anticipated was there. By the time

Rudy came along, Sophie and Dorotea were easy companions. Then, one morning in an elevator of the Deutsche Bank building, Rodolfo Bluhm unexpectedly slumped to the floor in the grip of a fatal heart attack. Within a few weeks, Carlos Bluhm had moved his little family into the big house to comfort his heartsick mother. It was then that Sophie became a loving and attentive daughter to Dorotea—a pillar in her bewildering world. As much as Dorotea loved her only son, she grew more committed, more connected to her daughter-in-law.

Bluhm went to sleep that night filled with happiness. His pilsner was curing in two copper vats. His mother was in her eiderdown bed, having floated upstairs on a current of good cheer. His son had retired to his books, carrying a full mug of steaming coffee. And when at last Bluhm crawled into bed, there was Sophie, sleeping peacefully in the lamplight, her face translucent and otherworldly—a book in her hands.

Why would a man in that familial paradise wake up the next morning with an irresistible itch to see another woman? It was a question for Oscar, the psychiatrist, if Bluhm had wanted to ask it. But Oscar was as much a philanderer as he was—ready to join a debauchery at the slightest provocation. Granted, no one could match Marco, the most flagrant of all the friends. Marco was insatiable, irredeemable—an ace voluptuary—a regular at Doña Felicia's infamous bordello on Twentieth Street, taking multiple whores in a single night. The real puzzlement was Willy, who insisted on keeping Carmela in that dump they called an apartment in San Borja—an insane expense for a man with five children. At least Oscar and Marco and Bluhm understood that sex was, after all, just sex, an indulgence that didn't have to unravel the family fabric or drain anybody's bank account.

Perhaps it was fear that Willy's profligacy would rub off on Bluhm that had prompted Sophie to snap at her husband with such uncharacteristic fury. She didn't need to. Bluhm understood perfectly well that his dalliances were passing fancies, easily discarded. The receptionist at *El Comercio* hadn't grasped this. Bluhm didn't want to enter into a messy, interminable liaison with a mistress. He couldn't afford to: not financially, not emotionally, and certainly not by any measure of the clock. He didn't want to spend the amount of time it took to tend to the likes of Carmela. If he had talked any of this through with Oscar, the doctor might have suggested to Bluhm that that was exactly why he had a fetish for the darker race. It wasn't the fragrant skin, the tiny toes, the thick black hair. An Indian woman was more disposable. It was a matter of convenience. And Bluhm's friends understood this about him very well.

WHEN WILLY AND CARMELA finally arrived at Lima Nights, Bluhm could hardly hide his displeasure. They were more than an hour late. Marco was sitting to Bluhm's side, already drunk and blowing kisses at a red-ribbon goddess on the dance floor. The woman looked back over her partner's shoulder with her lips slightly pursed, like a child trying to decide what to do.

Oscar took the cigar from his mouth and tamped it into the ashtray. "We're fucked, boys!" he said. "Just look around. The good ones are taken. We're flat on our asses, and here comes the sacred cow."

Carmela hurried toward them with her usual brass and bustle. Being of mixed race, she was taller than most women in the room. She was cinnamon-haired, buxom—attributes that helped disguise the plain woman she really was. Her wrists were thick, as were her ankles, but she had a certain confidence, a way of leaning in, fingering her hair, crossing one little foot over the other, as if she had it on good authority that she was a great beauty. Which Willy always took pains to assure her she was.

There was, Bluhm felt, something deeply repellent about her, in physicality as well as spirit. She was jovial, but excessively so, filling the air with raucous laughter. She was exaggerated in every way: too loud, too richly painted, too heavily perfumed, too turned out in flounces and bangles for a woman past counting her years. Bluhm had often wondered how his best friend had fallen into the clutches of such a harridan. But they had been paramours for almost a decade now—he couldn't dismiss the possibility that Willy was in love.

"You mad at us? Yes or no?" Carmela said, dropping herself into a chair, arms akimbo. "You look buzzed as a hornet, Bluhm. What a face!"

"No, darling," Willy hastened to say, patting her hand solicitously. "Bluhm isn't angry. He knows what the traffic can be like at this hour! Isn't that so, Carlos?"

"Of course," Bluhm said, swatting the smoke between them. But he was furious, it was true—at their lateness, at the woman's insufferable coarseness, at Marco's drunkenness, at the insistent drone of the bandoneón and the simpering cry of the tango singer. But there was this greatest of aggravations: The woman he was looking for was nowhere in the room. He had counted eleven red velvet collars, and not one announced the face he had come to see.

"What will you have, sweetness?" Willy asked Carmela, wiping his forehead with a rumpled handkerchief.

"Kir royale. In a flute. With a sprig of fresh chamomile."

It was a pathetic charade, the woman's attempt at sophistication, and it upped the amperage of Bluhm's irritation. It would have been churlish to begrudge Willy the comforts of a mistress. Bluhm simply couldn't understand how anyone could spend week after week with that intolerable woman at his side.

Willy Brenner had been his closest companion for thirty-five years—as smart and funny a friend as anyone could want. They had started at Swiss school together, gone off to the prestigious School of Engineers. And then, after one year, for all their families' lofty aspirations, the two had flunked out spectacularly. They were wealthy young men after a good time, confident in their boundless good fortunes. For years, the consonance between them continued: They both fell short of the glories their fathers had imagined for them; both married good women who gave them good children; and then, as years passed, both found themselves in crimped financial circumstances with substantial households to support. One had become a camera importer, the other a life-insurance salesman. They were not wealthy physicians like Oscar, with a full-time chauffeur and prosperous patients. Nor were they weekly fixtures on the society page, as was the gregarious hotelier Marco. Brenner and Bluhm were of another breed entirely. They were balding men in straitened circumstances—sybarites on the other side of splendor, grabbing at pleasures as they came.

No sooner had Willy and Carmela arrived than Bluhm carried his impatience to the shabby bar, where the manager—a gaunt little man with brilliantined hair—was in close consultation with the bartender. Bluhm tapped him vigorously on the shoulder. The manager spun around, displeased, but his bad humor quickly dissipated when he saw the neat jacket, crisp shirt, shiny wristwatch. "Jose Ferrari, at your service," he said, unctuously offering a hand.

"Juana Maria Fernandez," Bluhm responded.

The man stared back at him, puzzled.

"Where is she?"

"I have no idea who you mean."

"She's about this high. Long black hair. Goes by the name of Maria. She's one of your dancers in red nooses."

The man's lips pursed. "And you don't see her here?"

"No."

"But, señor, we have any number of pretty girls. If the one you're looking for isn't here, surely one of the—"

"Never mind!" Bluhm snapped, although in a far corner of consciousness, the same thought had occurred to him. Why, precisely, did it have to be Maria Fernandez? What was it about her that had held on like a bad cold? He was a man among friends, out for a good time. Why couldn't it be with any one of those other, perfectly satisfactory young women? But the thought did not stop him from heading for the door.

It was cool when he stepped outside, one of those petulant spring evenings in the last days of November when the frigid air over the Pacific rushes in over the southern hemisphere, deferring all dreams of an early summer. He turned his collar against the damp. Three blocks away, he found a public telephone. Taking the scrap of paper and a few coins from his pocket, he dialed the number.

He looked around as the phone rang. He was in a colorless part of town—it might have been any busy intersection in a busy district. Across the way, a neon sign extolling *Cerveza Cristal* flickered in a store window. It slid languidly from red to yellow, casting an unearthly glow on pedestrians as they hurried, nameless and golden, through the night.

"Hello?" It was a man's voice —young, gruff. Bluhm weighed his options quickly.

"I'm calling Juana Maria Fernandez," he said. And then added: "Jose Ferrari, the manager of Lima Nights."

The man grunted. "She's not here. What's the problem? She in some kind of trouble?"

"Trouble? No, no. I just need to talk to her, that's all." Bluhm paused. "About her hours."

"I don't know nothing about her hours, boss. Girl comes and goes like a ghost."

"Forgive me. Is this . . . her husband?"

"Ha!" The voice dissolved into a rolling chortle. Bluhm

frowned into the bracing wind, pulling his jacket close around him. "She's big for her age, I'll grant you that, Señor Ferrari. But, no, she hasn't managed to score a husband yet." Then, like an afterthought: "She's fifteen."

Bluhm hunched into the cold, factoring that piece of news, scrolling the sum total of everything he knew about Juana Maria Fernandez through the slow mill of comprehension: her black dress, full breasts, high heels—that sweet, sonorous voice of a siren.

"Hallo. You still there?"

He collected himself. "Yes."

"You want to leave a message? I've heard a lot of good stuff about your bar, señor. Nice place, eh? Good music?"

"Of course." And then it was out of his mouth before he could weigh the consequences: "Take down this number, please. Tell her to call me. Tell her I want to shift her schedule—my son Fritz has worked out the hours. She'll understand."

Walking back through the humid night, Bluhm felt numb, weighed down, as if something heavy had invaded his gut. Fifteen! Didn't they have laws against that in this country? She was younger than Fritz. Younger than Rudy! Younger than he would have imagined any checkout girl at Santa Isabel could be, much less a dancer at an adult bar. And what was she doing stuffing her telephone number into pockets of men three times her age?

It was a measure of how cruel life could be in this wretched city. The girl needed the work, needed to eat. But even as he grappled with the logic of that rationalization, he couldn't keep his mind off the result: the red mouth, the knowing eyes, the artful hips, the confident way she had taken his hands. But those images were altered now, as if he were summoning them through shattered glass.

By the time he made it back to the bar, his friends were all on the dance floor. Marco was with the beauty he'd been eyeing, stumbling as best he could through the complicated steps. Willy and Carmela were rocking to the music, locked in ridiculous embrace. Oscar and a woman in green satin were making their way to the bar, their faces lit with laughter. His three friends seemed happy, carefree, blissfully unaware or, at least, unconcerned about his whereabouts. *"Vivir!"* the singer warbled. *"Con el alma aferrada a un dulce recuerdo, que lloro otra vez!"*

He called over Jose Ferrari, paid his bill, and left.

2

Maria

THE MOMENT SHE SAW THE MESSAGE SCRAWLED on a corner of her mother's laundry book, she ran to the back of the house. It was late, a little past one in the morning, but the words written in her brother's hand—*Call your boss. Fritz worked it out*, followed by an unfamiliar number—propelled her to her brothers' door.

"Freddy!" she called as she burst into the room. Her brother groaned and rolled over.

"Did you write this?" she said, shaking the notebook in his face. "Wake up! I need to know!"

"Shut your mouth!" came a voice from the dark.

"Shut up yourself, Pablito. I'm not talking to you, asshole."

Freddy propped himself up on one elbow. "For the love of God, it's the goddamn middle of the night. What's so important?"

"I'm sorry, Freddy." She lowered her voice to a whisper and knelt down beside his cot. "But what does it mean?"

He slumped back onto his pillow. "Your boss at the bar. He called and said that Fritz changed all the schedules. You're not in trouble. He wants you to call back, that's all."

She lay in bed, puzzling over her boss, the unfamiliar number, Fritz. The grease-head had called her at home? There was no way he could have known that number—a public telephone just outside their door. But more important, Jose Ferrari never told his dancers whether or not there was work. You showed up at six-thirty, at which point he'd tell you to stick around or scram. The night before, she'd gone with her dress and shoes in a bag, as she always did, only to be told she wasn't needed. It didn't make sense that he would call a few hours later to talk about schedules.

Then there was Fritz. The only Fritz she'd ever heard of, apart from those dumb jokes her mother's lover liked to tell, was the tall, sloppy kid who had come to the supermarket with the white guy. The one with the penetrating eyes. Suddenly it all made sense. The note she had tucked into his pocket had worked, just as one of the bargirls had said it would. Staring at the cement walls of her tiny room, she hardly slept for the hope mounting in her heart.

The cock crowed, and soon she heard her mother drag the big laundry basin out to the back stoop to begin the day's work. Then came the whoosh of water from a pail one of her brothers had filled the night before. It was Friday, the busiest day of the week, and people would soon be depositing their dirty clothes, wanting them clean and crisp before Sunday. She heard a sharp report as a hard object rebounded off the aluminum basin.

"Jesus!" her mother shouted. "What the hell did that prick carry in that pocket? A goddamn rock?" Only months ago, Berta Fernandez would have roused Maria from dead slumber to help with the reeking piles, but now that her girl was earning good money, she let her sleep, shushing her boys if they so much as raised their voices. "Has it ever occurred to you fat-ass losers that it's us with the tits who bring home the cash?" she'd hiss at them. "You can't find a job to save your lives, but that little girl, who's smarter than both of you put together, has *two*."

The night before, when Maria had been told she wasn't needed at Lima Nights, she had taken a jitney to the supermarket and begged the night manager to let her work the late shift. "Please, Robertito," she'd begged. "I'll sweep the floors, clean out the back, do whatever you say. I need the money, Fats." He was a big oaf, easy to charm, especially when she kidded him along, let him think he might fish his thick paw down her blouse.

By the time she'd taken the last bus home, trying to beat the government's new one o'clock curfew, she was wrung out. She had trouble keeping her eyes open as she stumbled along the dirt road to the house, but she clasped the purse with her evening's pay tight to her chest and kept an eye on the alley-ways. High on the hill, she could see the flickering lights of the prison. When she turned the corner onto her little road, her eyes finally lit on home: a cement box with a corrugated tin roof like any other, except for the hand-painted sign over the door: WASHERWOMAN. She unlocked the bolt, headed straight for the kitchen, and flicked on the bulb to see if she could hunt up some bread, ease the ache in her belly—and suddenly there it was, a number scribbled on her mother's ledger, like a light from another world.

At ten, she padded outside and made the call. A woman's voice answered, "Hello?"

"This is Juana Maria Fernandez," she said.

"And to whom do you wish to speak?"

"Fritz."

"He's not here, señorita," the woman said. "He's already left for the university. How can I help you?"

"How about the señor? Is he there?"

"No. He's at *El Comercio* today."

Maria hesitated.

"And Mrs. Bluhm, too, is out doing errands," the woman said. "Are you one of Fritz's friends? I'm sorry I don't recognize your name, but so many young people are always calling! Would you like to leave a message?"

She placed the receiver on the hook gently. So, his name was Bluhm. He was somehow connected to the newspaper and rich enough to have a maid—a very good one. And he had been smart enough to leave a coded message. It was just as the older women at Lima Nights had always said it would be: The best customers—the ones you should keep your eyes open for—were a little twisted, a little hungry, and very, very cautious. No, Mr. Bluhm wasn't slow-footed at all.

She went to her room, closed the door and sat on the edge

of the cot, gazing around at the tiny cubicle. The rusty clock told her she had an hour and a half before she was expected at the supermarket. Above it, on a sturdy hook, hung the four tango dresses her mother had sewn for her: red, white, black, and a shimmering electric blue. There was a table Freddy had fashioned from wood he'd accumulated from the garbage hills, and, on it, her dead father's shaving mirror, her magic amulets, and three spiral notebooks from school. Across, on the grimy sill of a barred window, sat the pink lockbox where she kept the money. Its corners were brown with rust, but inside was a neat little stack, which she'd been putting aside for months. All the rest had gone for household expenses.

She looked down at her toes, still dusty from the road. Her spine ached from endless hours of lugging boxes. Studying her fingers, she saw that two nails were broken. Wearily, she rose to begin her day's ritual. She went out to the stoop, kissed her mother good morning, filled a tin basin with water from one of the pails, and started back to her room to wash her face. Somewhere in the distance she could hear her brothers shouting—a spirited, happy exchange, followed by the thwap of an improvised rag ball against a shoe. Just as she passed the front door, the telephone rang in the street. She set the basin on the floor hastily, splashing cold water onto her feet.

The man on the other end of the line recognized her voice immediately. "Maria," he said. "Is that you?"

"Mr. Bluhm," she said.

There was a long pause and then he spoke again. "I want to see you. Only briefly. There's something I need to say. And something I need to see."

She told him to meet her at five in front of the Santa Isabel. "It's in your neighborhood, no?"

"Not far."

"I have a bit of time after work before I need to be at the bar."

"A bit of time is all we'll need."

She felt her heart race as she searched the crates under her cot for something to wear. Santa Isabel employees were not allowed to leave the premises in uniform, but it wouldn't do to appear in tango costume in full daylight on a busy street in San Isidro, and those four dresses were the only good clothes she had. She folded a white shirt and a pair of black slacks into a bag and, after a little thought, tossed in a tube of bright lipstick and her patent-leather dancing shoes. She straightened her bed quickly, took two crisp bills from her pink box, and hurried out into the sun.

She thought of little else for five hours as she bustled about the supermarket. Her colleagues were good-humored, full of banter, but when she wasn't stuffing bags and attending to customers, she couldn't bring herself to pay them much mind. She sat on a stool and gazed into the distance, wondering what Bluhm would say.

Monica, the oldest dancer at Lima Nights—the one with the wild black hair and eyes ringed with fatigue—always said that the smartest girls knew when to listen. It was fine to laugh, tell jokes, flirt with a man, but there came a time when he might want something more than an armful of warm woman: You had to watch for those moments, open your eyes and ears. The girls who listened, she said, who made men feel important, were the ones who would move up in this lousy world—become their lovers, spend the rest of their days lounging in apartments with real bathrooms, shiny refrigerators, soft beds. "You have a brain, Maria," Monica would say to her. "You're not like the others. You know how to talk, how to impress a man. But what you need to learn now is how to listen."

It was the first time she'd ever slipped a telephone number into a man's pocket. Not that she hadn't had her share of experience. She'd had sex at twelve, courtesy of one of her mother's many lovers—men who blew in and out of their house freely. The rape had been quick, painful, incomprehensible. But as her breasts and hips had begun to ripen, she learned that the mere promise of sex could give a girl power. She played at it after that, allowing herself to be fondled, and then taken in an abandoned shack by a strong boy of fourteen, but she quickly understood that she could not afford to be reckless. It was a lesson her mother had unintentionally taught: Give too much too often and you squander your value in the marketplace of men. Her mother was a good woman, a hard worker, but her appetite for sex had been their undoing, a family curse, really: costing her husband his life, her sons their pride, Maria her innocence, making them all a target of cruel gossip in their benighted hillside inferno.

Strange, how something in that man's face—in those lively blue eyes and courtly air—had made her feel safe and comfortable. As if he'd been on his way to her all along. Perhaps he was her man from another universe, as a fortune-teller had once put it: The one who would rescue her from misfortune. The one who would keep her from harm.

AT FIRST BLUHM DIDN'T recognize her. She looked like any number of young women emerging purposefully from the grocery store. She was wearing a tidy white shirt, black pants, high heels, geranium-pink lipstick, and her hair was pulled into a sleek ponytail. He'd been looking for a girl of fifteen.

Not until she was directly before him did he realize she was the person he'd come to see. That moment of lightning comprehension left him at a rare loss for words. She put out one hand, and when he took it, she clasped his with both, as if she were the genial host, putting her visitor at ease. She told him there was a clean pastry shop around the corner, where they could sit, drink coffee.

Once they got there, he surprised himself by offering her a cigarette. He wanted one desperately. She took it, allowed him to light it for her, and sat back, inhaling deeply. "I've been looking forward to seeing you, señor," she said, releasing the truth and the smoke all at once.

"Please, don't call me that. You make me feel like a fossil. Just call me—"

"Carlos," she said. "Carlos Bluhm."

"Yes. How do you know?"

"Your maid! She's very efficient. She told me your last name. The first I got from your friends the night we met."

She seemed extraordinarily self-assured for a young person. He couldn't imagine his own sons, who had had the benefit of good schools and breeding, in similar conversation with a stranger. It was eerie, that kind of poise in a child.

"Well, I was too drunk that night to remember much of anything," he said, straightening. "But I got sober fast when I got home and found your number in my pocket."

"Really? Why?"

"You're fifteen, for God's sake!"

"Sixteen very soon!" she raised her voice to match his. "And who told you, anyway?"

"It doesn't matter!" He glanced at the face behind the counter and saw the man's look of alarm. "Listen," Bluhm said, dropping his voice to a near whisper. "Now that we're here, do me the courtesy of listening to me, please." She was looking at him with wide eyes, her slick pink lips slightly parted. "I've seen what I came to see," he said with a wave of his hand. "You're every bit as lovely today as you were that night, as you were that other day in the supermarket. You're a beautiful girl, Maria. I wanted to see you again, and I don't mean to lick ice cream cones on the Malecón, understand? It's a good thing that your pocket trick brought you here, to this little pastry shop with me, and not into the claws of some lecher." He reached across and grabbed her by the wrist. "You're a child! I realize the law only requires you to be in school until you're thirteen, and I know very well that you're working two jobs—maybe even helping to support your family. But for the love of God, watch out—men will take what they want from you and throw whatever's left to the hills of

Lurigancho. Don't be stupid!" His eyes were dark now, filled with anger. "Sticking your number into strangers' pockets! How crazy can you get?" He tapped his forehead for emphasis. Then he leaned back and stubbed out his cigarette.

"Is that what you came here to say?"

"Yes, it is."

She took a sip of her espresso, studying him over the rim of her cup. "I've never given that telephone number to anyone else. You are the first." A look of disbelief crossed his face. "I'm not as dumb as you think, Carlos. I know exactly what I'm doing," she went on evenly. "As for having some man throw me to the heaps of Lurigancho: Lurigancho is where I live. Right there, by the prison, with all the sick lechers of Lima. My father's dead. My brothers are out of work. My mother is driving herself to an early grave. I'm not on a dangerous road, headed for perdition. I'm there already."

She was speaking softly, but her eyes were fierce. He crossed his arms, amazed.

"You live around here, don't you?" she continued. "Here in San Isidro, where the air smells of perfume. You have no idea what it's like for someone to go back and forth from the slum where I live. Day after day, week after week. The dirt, the barbed wire, the stink. Watch out for men? What do you know about me?" She didn't wait for an answer. "Nothing! You know nothing! Now, let me say what I've come to say, señor, and you listen to me like the big grown-up you are. I liked you the moment I laid eyes on you. I liked your friendly face, your eyes, the way you looked at me, the way you seemed to like what you saw. I'm no genius. You're right, I have the minimum education by law—not a day over the eighth grade. And I suppose that means I'm not good enough to deserve your attention. Not your pity, mind you. And not your concern for my safety. Your *attention*. That's what I want. As a man. For a woman."

She got up, pushed in her chair, and walked away.

EARLY THE NEXT MORNING, she went to the telephone company on Avenida Arequipa. She lifted one of the heavy directories from its chain, placed it on the long wooden counter, and consulted the listings for Lima and its surrounding suburbs. Skimming her finger down the page, she found what she was looking for: *BLUHM von Roedenbeck CARLOS*. The address was *300 Av. Rivera, San Isidro*. The telephone number matched the one she'd called. Checking the map on the wall, she saw that Avenida Nicolás de Rivera ran parallel to the Golf Club and perpendicular to San Isidro's famous avenues: Conquistadores, Libertadores, and the Camino Real. Carefully, she wrote down the information she would need to get there.

At five o'clock, she took off her uniform, placed it tidily on its hanger in the women's service room, changed, and left, heading for the Camino Real. She was surprised at how short the walk was to Bluhm's street, but in less than ten minutes she was gazing up at a green sign engraved with bold white letters: *Nic. de Rivera*. It was a quiet neighborhood, with an armed guard posted on every corner; a colossus of a man in a gold-braided uniform kept vigil by the Boutique de Paris. Turning the corner from Salamanca, she saw that there were no more shops ahead, only mansions circled by wrought-iron fences or high stucco walls. The house at 300 Rivera was on the left. Visible behind an ornate gate, it was nestled in a lush garden of flowers. The massive walls were a fresh, bright white; the roof, rippling waves of terra-cotta. The polished wood of the front door seemed to mirror the wood of the intricately carved balcony. A low wall of brightly painted tiles circled the house's perimeter. It wasn't the largest structure on the street, by any means, but it struck her as the most pleasing. From where she stood, she could see a white brocade couch in the living room, a black piano with its wing in the air. In the entryway was a marble table displaying a gigantic vase of sunflowers. With its windows open and door ajar, the house seemed to be smiling, beckoning her in.

"You!" a voice called behind her. She whirled around to see a soldier, in full green regimentals, crossing the street, a gun slung over his shoulder. He was short, square—his face riddled with pockmarks. "Yes, you!" he shouted, walking more briskly now. "You have business here?"

She shook her head. Clearly, she looked out of place in this white man's paradise. "No, no," she said, as ingratiatingly as she could, noting the surname on his shirt. "I'm sorry to have alarmed you, Officer Pérez, but I've been offered a job in this house and I was only walking by to see if I'd be happy living and working here. They're not expecting me. I just meant to go past for a quick look."

The soldier's face softened. "Oh, I see." He smiled genially, pushed his cap off his forehead, and offered the prospective maid an opinion. "Well, I think you'd like it, señorita. I've been posted here for a few weeks, and this part of San Isidro is very pleasant. It's a safe neighborhood. Peaceful. Not much goes on, apart from the occasional party. And the gringos in that house are fairly quiet. They keep to themselves. From time to time, I hear music. The fancy kind. You know. Like you hear in movies."

She nodded.

"Forgive me for being so abrupt just now," he added, "but you know how it is these days with terrorists about and so many bombs going off around the city. The army can't be too careful. Anyone who looks like they don't belong here? Well . . . we just have to ask."

TEN DAYS WENT BY before Bluhm saw her again. It took that long for spring to become summer, for the life around them to gather pulse and flower. The floripondio dangled white blossoms into the warm air; women shrugged off their wraps and bared their shoulders; even the belligerents of the Shining Path, who all winter long had flung Molotov cocktails through bank windows, seemed to relent, as if the sun had coaxed forth their better natures.

Summer brought Christmas too, which meant that Bluhm's sales commissions were up. By the tenth of December he received a check from the Zeiss headquarters in Germany, which included a small bonus. On the same sun-filled day, he did his Christmas shopping—a silk mantilla for Dorotea, a bottle of Arpège for Sophie, a tennis racquet for Fritz, a miniature billiards game for Rudy. As he was driving home, feeling the liberality of the season, he resolved to go that very evening to Lima Nights.

He hadn't been able to put her out of his mind. Every time a young woman with long black hair passed on the street, he strained to see her features. If a jitney darted by with *Lurigancho* painted on its flank, he would search its passengers, hoping to find her. They seemed a miserable lot, packed into those vans—the poor, the dead-eyed, shuttling between his world and hers. But he hardly factored them. His mind was on her face: the heart-shaped chin, the vivid lips, the umber skin, the nose that flared ever so slightly when she listened. More than anything—as he lay in bed, waiting for sleep to come—he remembered her eyes. The passion that raged there. The fury. He wondered if she'd turned sixteen.

He left shortly after eight, telling Sophie he had a pressing business engagement. By nine he was in the tango bar, watching her dance. She was swinging her hips at a grinning fool, her face radiant, her gaudy blue dress illuminated by winking lights. When the music stopped, she saw him. He was the only white there apart from Jose Ferrari, and in that vast room with few customers, his face had been easy to spot. She excused herself and made her way toward his table.

"I knew you'd come," she said, placing both hands on the wood.

"Sit, sit. Join me for a drink. Can you?"

She looked around. "If you buy me hard liquor. That's the

rule." He waved over a waiter and ordered her a rum and Coke.

They tried to chat over the din of the music, but the tango was insistent and, before long, he shouted, "Let's go where we can talk. I have something to give you."

She shouted back, "I can't. If I leave, Jose won't pay me."

"How much?"

She told him. It was less than he'd paid for lunch.

"I'll give it to you," he said.

She ran off to change, and when they met on the street she was in jeans and a striped polo shirt. Except for the red lips, the girl looked very much her age.

They walked to a nearby *chifa,* where a man and a woman were sitting out in the pleasant night air, dipping fried wontons into tamarind sauce. Bluhm offered her a chair. A Chinese man in a white coat brought them two glasses of frothy papaya punch.

"When's your birthday?" he asked after they'd ordered a plate of shrimp.

"Next week." She was pleased to see he'd remembered it and gave him all the benefit of her smile. "On Wednesday." She took a long sip of her drink, and the sight of that heartbreaking mouth pursed around the straw tugged at something in the pit of his stomach. Her arms were the color of cinnamon bark, her shoulders small and delicate under the child's shirt. She brushed the bangs out of her eyes and he could see a cluster of tiny pimples over one brow, as curved as a crescent moon. He took a little package from his pocket and placed it on the table in front of her.

"I might as well give this to you now."

"What is it?"

"A birthday present. Open it!"

She tore into the box, ripping away the paper, pulling off the top as if she were releasing the contents from long, unhappy bondage. It was a black organdy necklace, hung with a silver heart. She draped it around her throat, laughing—"It's beautiful. Beautiful!"—broadcasting her joy so spiritedly that the waiter came around to see.

They talked on for two hours after that, taking their time over an enormous heap of shrimp and fried rice. She told him about her house by the prison, a tiny box with a metal roof that was suffocating in summer, piercingly damp in winter. A hive of those hovels had sprouted like fungus when the chief warden had announced that an army of laborers would be needed to wash the uniforms, cook the food, and guard the one million thugs who passed annually through the prison doors. It was the only house she had ever known.

She told him then about her dream to live in an old mansion in San Isidro, complete with a black piano and a lush, fragrant garden. He wondered at the coincidence of that, and then, to change the subject, told her about a pipe dream of his own: to write a history of the Bluhms, starting with the family's origins in Europe.

"But you write all the time, don't you? At the newspaper?"

He laughed. "I don't work for a newspaper, sweetheart. I can't imagine where you got that idea. Although I'll admit, next month I hope to get a fat commission on a sale of cameras to *El Comercio*."

She marveled at how selling cameras could make a man so rich. After a while, she said, "Why don't you go to a *vidente*, Carlos? He'll tell you whether or not your dream will come true."

"A fortune-teller? Psshh! I don't go in for that sort of thing."

"Well," she speared a shrimp with her fork, "all I can tell you is that one read my fortune, and it turned out to be exactly as he said."

"Oh? And how did he do that?" he asked, humoring her.

She popped the shrimp into her mouth, pulled her bag from the chair beside her, and drew out a blue velvet pouch, no larger than the cup of her hand. Loosening the drawstring, she shook its contents onto the table. A crude metal crucifix tumbled out, carved with the image of a dove—its heart punctured by a red pebble. Behind it, a cheap aluminum ring, with a raised blue stone. "These are my lucky amulets," she said. "They made what he said come true." She looked up and explained. "He said that a man would come from another universe. That he would rescue me, take me from all my troubles. He told me this man would swallow my shark."

"Shark?"

"It's an old Indian saying," she said. "The shark is the ache in your belly. The thing that eats at you from the inside." She held out the trinkets, beaming sweetly. "You know what I think?" she said, taking his hand and dropping the objects gently into his palm so that the ring hit the cross with the sharp click of finality.

He shook his head.

"I think my man from that other universe is you."

JOSE FERRARI WAS FURIOUS when Maria appeared the next night, bag in hand, looking to be chosen. "You! Why should I ever use you again?" he said, his face beaked as a bird's. "I give you work and what do you do? Skip out and take my customer!"

"No, Jose, please. I promise I won't do it again. And, besides, I was only making sure he'd come back. Believe me, he will."

"I see," he said. "So you went out and fucked him?"

"No!"

"You know the rules!" he shouted. "All of you!" He glared at the small gathering of women. "No fucking the customers, understand? I want my customers here! I want them ordering drinks and piqueos! I'm a restaurant man, not a pimp."

She held her tongue. But she could see that he would need her tonight—there were far too few women in the room. She took her long hair, pulled it over one shoulder, and shifted her weight to the other hip.

"Okay," he sighed. "Show me what you've got there." She lifted her bag and pulled out the red tube dress with the white appliqué hearts. He squinted at it, then nodded. "Put it on."

Next morning at the supermarket was just as frustrating. Robertito, the night manager, had been switched to day, and a number of his workers wanted to switch with him. Agreeing to take two, he was trying to decide which of the regular day workers would compensate by moving to the night shift. Someone suggested Maria.

She argued her case in tears, pleading with him to keep her where she was. She had a night job already, she explained, and her family desperately needed the money. Changing her shift would be ruinous. The fat man thrust out his lip in a feigned pout and said, "Ay, ay, ay! What a sob story! And so, little girl, what do you propose to do for me in exchange?"

"Whatever you say, Robertito," she answered, wiping her eyes. He patted her on the rump and sent her to change into her uniform.

It seemed her troubles had ended, at least for the time being, until she returned home that same day, after a long night at the tango bar. Her mother was in the kitchen—drunk—a cigarette in one hand, a glass of cheap aguardiente in the other. Her forehead was marred by a purple gash, and Maria could see the dried trail of blood that had coursed down her neck to her dress. Freddy and Pablito were nowhere to be found. Nor was her mother's lover.

"That man is worse than your father ever was!" her mother shouted. "What a jealous prick! I was only talking to someone, for Chrissake, handing an asshole his shirts! I can't be blamed for what some sonofabitch says to me! Or if he pinches my ass!"

It wasn't the first time he had given her a good thrashing. But it was the first he had drawn blood.

Maria cleaned her mother's wound and led her to bed,

where she undressed her carefully and pulled a sheet over her thin frame. At thirty-seven, Berta Fernandez was an old woman with a child's body—flat in all the places a woman should be round. To look at her lying there, helpless, was surely to look at the least desirable woman in the world. But, for all her deficiencies, Berta was catnip to the males of Lurigancho. Maybe it was her face, with its sloe lynx eyes. Or maybe it was her mouth, which was foul and funny, a veritable fount of obscenities. She was lewd in the extreme. And she was incorrigible, fueled by a constant hunger. It had always been so—the drinking too much, the loud fornication behind closed doors, the fleeing through the nights, nude. She was as feral as a cat. The question had always been: How badly would things end? Maria's father had been killed one night when she was five. Knife in hand, he'd made a run for the bare back of one of his wife's lovers. But the lover had been more agile, a powerful young guard from the prison. He simply twisted the blade in the direction from which it came and plunged it into her father's heart, killing him instantly. The judge ruled murder in self-defense and the lover was free to move into the house, where for months he held court in the dead man's bedroom, even as the children grieved. In time, her mother found someone new, the youth was turned out, and the people of Lurigancho began to cover their mouths when she passed and whisper about her ill-starred children.

Maria's head was pounding as she crawled into her narrow cot. The peace she had felt as her bus rumbled through the dark had been mere illusion. Her mother would never change. Someday the woman would get herself killed, and where would Berta Fernandez's sons be then? Kicking the stones down some dusty alley, whiling away the hours—marking time until God Himself reached down and put them all out of their misery.

She stared up into the night, feeling the resolute beat of her heart. Two more days and she would be sixteen. Only two more and she would see Bluhm again. But even a short span from dusk to dawn seemed an eternity. She felt unmoored, as if she'd been whirled out on the dance floor with nothing to hold on to. Nothing but music and air.

3

Carlos

HE SPED DOWN THE STREET A FEW MINUTES BE-fore the appointed hour and was surprised to find her there, on the corner of Camino Real and Bustamante, looking about nervously, registering every car that went by.

It was one of Lima's torrid summer afternoons when the air in the city seemed to stand still, and, as she climbed into the passenger's seat, he could see she was perspiring. She smelled of lemons and salt. Beads of moisture clung to her upper lip and forehead, and the whites of her eyes, which had always shone from the deep brown of her face, were shot through with red. Bluhm wondered if she had a slight fever.

He wondered, too, why she appeared so disoriented; she seemed to hesitate at every turn—not quite able to shut the door, sitting stiffly away from the seat, glancing about at the conveniences that surrounded her. There, in her sleeveless white top and short denim skirt, she seemed the very opposite of the smart, confident girl he had sat with at the *chifa*. She looked a little worn, a little worried.

Bluhm pointed to the neatly wrapped package on the front seat, and she managed a wan smile before turning back to the window. He had brought two portions of her favorite dessert, a flan made of dulce de leche, just as he had said he would. But she seemed incapable of appreciating the gesture or making small talk, and so the box lay between them like a stone.

He drove to a scruffy park in Miraflores, far from his house and far from the neighborhood of anyone he knew. Swinging the old black Peugeot through the narrow streets, trying to avoid potholes, he was deeply aware of their intimate proximity. They had never been this close, this alone, and for a fleeting moment they seemed to be two warm-blooded animals, trapped in metal, passing the breath of life between them. He glanced down at her bare legs and saw that she had wedged her hands between her knees. Her thick hair hung down, grazing her thighs. Her shoulders were slightly raised, slightly on guard, but her nearness was animating. A longing rose through his groin.

They found a bench under a peppertree whose berries were just beginning to ripen. A flock of tiny white butterflies danced by, brushing their wings against bark. The fresh air, green grass, blue sky seemed to revive her momentarily. She breathed deeply, leaned back into the bench, and closed her eyes.

They talked a little about her birthday after that, but it was a day like any other. She had worked all morning and afternoon and, except for this hour in this nameless park, she would be working all night. She ate her flan listlessly, licking the burnt sugar from a plastic fork and looking out at the distance as if the ghost of something were gathering there.

"You seem preoccupied," he said. "Where's the happy birthday girl?"

She turned and studied his face. "Make no mistake, Carlos," she said at last. "I'm very grateful for all you do. The dinner at the *chifa*, the pretty necklace, the birthday flan. It's all very generous. Very kind. But, since you ask, here's what preoccupies me: Why are you doing it? Am I a little charity case you've decided to take up so that I don't fall into the hands of some lecher, as you put it? What is it you want from me exactly?" But she gave him no chance to answer those questions. She forged ahead.

"I can't imagine you want my company. You have rich, fancy friends with far more interesting lives, who make better conversation. And you're not really serious about learning the tango, are you? Which, frankly, is the only thing on earth I do very well. I haven't danced it for long, but I do seem to have some skill for it. So what is it you want? My body? Sex? You haven't made a move. You want to touch? You want to feel? Here!"

She took his hand and slapped it on her thigh. "You've wanted to do that from the very first, haven't you? So what's stopping you? You said in the beginning that you didn't want to get to know me in order to lick ice cream cones in a park, but look at us! That's exactly what we're doing!"

He moved his fingers over her skin as if he were petting a fractious animal, noting the silk of its coat. "Maria," he said finally, taking his hand away, "I don't know what to tell you." And that was God's truth. He hadn't expected such directness. She was right that he had wanted sex with her. And, if he'd never been told her age, they might have had it by now. Still, knowing everything he did, he hadn't been able to move on, forget her. He was consumed, infatuated. A well of remorse filled his throat. "I'm sorry. I wanted to wish you a happy birthday, and all I've managed to do is make you angry."

"I'm not angry!" she cried. "I'm not," she repeated more softly. "Here's what I am: I'm sixteen. I have a few dreams. I may not know much. I'm not like your son—rich, smart, studying in a university. I've never been inside a car until today, until just now, with you. Don't you get it, Mr. Bluhm? You are white. I am Indian. You are rich. I am poor. You live in San Isidro and have ancestors you'd like to write about. I live in Lurigancho—I have no idea where my ancestors are from. The one thing we share is this." She touched one hand to his heart and then to her own. "This, Carlos—*this*. The most important thing. The thing between men and women."

He was stunned. How could a child be capable of such words? He could see now that she had been agonizing about this for days. That he was the reason for the red eyes, the serious mouth, the nervous air. More than anything now he wanted to stroke her legs, slip his hands under her skirt, squeeze the round fruit of her perfect breasts, which seemed to lift toward him like a question.

Instead, he reached out, folded the girl to his chest, and held her tight.

• • •.

CHRISTMAS CAME AND WENT, a mix of paralysis and frenzy. Bluhm would not be able to picture much of it when, many years later, he would be pressed to remember. But the facts were these: Even as Bluhm sat in his study and stared out the window, fixed by indecision, his oldest son finished his first year at the university with honors; his youngest performed Bach's *"Erbarme Dich"* at the Jubilee Concert at the Club Germania; and his wife extracted a promise from him to rent—if only for a week, and at the cheapest rate possible—a modest cottage in the seaside resort of Paracas. She argued that if the rental was late in the season, in early March, they might find a place they could afford.

Only three months before, they had been struggling to make ends meet. Sophie's strict discipline had gone a long way, but the burden of school tuitions had been punishing. Dorotea quietly began pawning the family silver. "We won't miss it. There's so much of the stuff, and it just sits in that old sideboard," she told Sophie in confidence. "Let me help you this way for a while, and when Fritz and Rudy are grown and prosperous, they can buy it all back for you." Those monthly trips to the silver merchants on La Paz, selling a pitcher here, a platter there, had certainly made Sophie's life easier. She had accumulated, by her reckoning, just enough to buy the family ten full days in that shining bower on the beach.

Dorotea was right: The silver wasn't missed. The finances were such that Sophie couldn't even contemplate entertaining during the holidays. No longer could she and Carlos host the large family gatherings with Riesling and gingerbread and Westphalian ham paraded by servants on gargantuan silver platters. Instead, Christmas Eve dinner was consumed in the vast, dank dining hall of the Westermanns, Sophie's parents, who lived in a suburb on the periphery of Lima; and Christmas Day lunch was hosted by Veronica von Roedenbeck, a spirited socialite on Carlos's side of the family. The Bluhms' financial predicament was not discussed openly among the members of the extended family, but it was understood: The Bluhms were to be invited out, the restaurant bills paid discreetly, and it went without saying that little would be expected in return.

One of the holiday affairs was in Oscar's grand house at the edge of the Malecón, overlooking the Pacific. The psychiatrist, who had been honored that week by the Academy of Physicians, was in fine form, holding forth on the follies of the country's new president and pouring liberally from festive magnums of imported champagne. Near the end of the party, when the guests were few and the women repaired to the terrace for coffee and gossip, Bluhm and his friends settled into the tan leather sofas in the living room to smoke their cigars.

"So, tell us, Willy," Marco began impishly, "what did Carmela get for Christmas? Did you give her that diamond she's been hankering for all these years?" He was handsome in his blue Italian blazer and tailored shirt.

"Oh, I don't know," Willy said, running his hand over his balding head, "a box of chocolates, something along those lines."

The wistfulness in his voice made Bluhm want to offer comfort. Despite his opinion of the woman, he heard himself say, "Christmases must be hard on the Carmelas of the world, what with the demands of family."

"The Carmelas of the World!" Oscar said, circling his cigar in the air. "Now, there's the title of a book for you!"

"Ha!" interjected Marco. "Short book! As far as I know, there's only one Carmela in this world! God help us!"

Willy looked at his friends wearily. Where was his sense of humor? "Leave Carmela alone, okay?" he said. "I don't need to be reminded how much you dislike her. I love her. I don't think I need to explain it." He folded his arms and sighed. "And as you all know, I love my wife and children too. This Christmas has been torture—wanting to be in two places at once. But there you are: It's the cancer I've inflicted on myself, my chronic illness. I don't need any of you to make it worse."

A rare, uncomfortable silence descended as the three glanced at one another, digesting their friend's wretchedness. "How about you, Bluhm?" Oscar said, trying to lighten the mood. "Any sugarplums in your stocking?"

Bluhm was struck momentarily by the question. Not by its suggestiveness or cheek, since the four of them had long ago reached a high tolerance for mutual mockery. He was struck by a sudden and burning desire to tell them about the girl.

"Yes, one," he said simply. "The dancer at Lima Nights."

"Which one?" they all asked at once.

"Maria. The one with the long black hair."

There was a second's hesitation before Marco blurted, "I remember her! She's the hot little monkey, no?"

"Oh, come on, Marco," Oscar said, licking the rim of his brandy glass. "Of course she's a monkey. We all know that about Bluhm, don't we? He has a nose for the *cholas*. Just like a good cup of coffee, eh? Short, sweet, and brown!" The psychiatrist chuckled, winking at Bluhm.

"She's sixteen years old."

"No!" Marco blurted, delighted. "That's sick, man!" But he was laughing and raising a glass. "She didn't look sixteen to me."

"She was fifteen when you saw her," Bluhm added.

"Jesus," somebody said. And then—silence. Bluhm looked around at the faces that confirmed his own unease.

"Oscar!" a woman's voice called brightly from the terrace. "Tell the boy to bring us some limoncello, will you, darling?"

"Yes, dear," Oscar called back, but he continued to stare at his friend. After what seemed a long while, he asked, "So, you fooled around with this girl?"

"Not in the way you think."

Marco raised an eyebrow and exchanged glances with Oscar. Willy seemed altogether stupefied.

"Well!" Marco said at last, clicking his cigar against an ashtray. "It's not her age that bothers me, frankly. I was fourteen when I did it for the first time. And my woman was thirty-five. So what's the difference? A few years on either side—a little switch of the genders. Sixteen? Go back a few generations and that was the age our grandmothers were when they married. What *does* bother me, though, is the race. What is it with you, Bluhm? Are you nuts? They're dirty, man! Dirty and dumb. You might as well do it with a goat."

"Now, now," said Willy, pushing himself to the edge of his seat. "You have no right to say that. I've seen you go through Doña Felicia's whorehouse like a worm through fruit. I don't see you checking the color of every butt you grab."

"Oh, my! Such a serious discussion!" It was Willy's wife, standing in the doorway—too far away to hear what was being said. "I was delegated to come and find out what happened to our limoncello, but it looks as if it's met with some heavy artillery! Are you gentlemen deciding the fate of the world?" Beatriz was rail thin in her gauzy blue dress, and it billowed behind her as she floated, laughing, toward the kitchen.

"You want my advice, Carlos?" Oscar offered, as soon as the door swung shut behind Beatriz. He was calm and clinical, tapping his knee with a finger. "Don't mess with children. I don't care what Marco says—in this enlightened age, a sixteen-year-old girl is a child. I don't know what you're up to, and honestly I don't want to know. I learned long ago not to put my nose into my friends' britches. But watch yourself, brother. I don't give a damn what happens to the *chola*. I'd like a centavo for every pretty girl who comes down from the sierra, looking for a white man to give her a good time. But I do give a damn what it could do to you."

BLUHM DIDN'T LISTEN.

Having his closest friends know about her was restorative—and, in a peculiar way, a license. He had told the truth, confessed. He had felt something akin to a blessing, an absolution, when they slapped him on the back and pressed him to their hearts as they moved, one by one, into the humid night. Never in his life had he felt he needed anyone's permission to do as he pleased with a woman, but there was something different about this transaction, something different about the girl. He left Oscar's house feeling light and disburdened, his appetite for her renewed.

In truth, nothing they could have said would have discouraged him. Not about her skin. Not about her age. He wanted to feel her in his arms again, hold her tight. It came to this: He wanted to look at her face, listen to that voice—the way she ripped every word from her heart. Of course, there was nothing for Oscar to worry about. The transaction between them would be quick, harmless, over soon. What had she called it? The hunger that gnawed at your gut? Something about a shark?

At nine the next morning, he called the number in Lurigancho. He knew it would be the right time, a full hour before she left for work. A hoarse female voice answered— high, raucous, and, at first, unintelligible. He had to repeat himself several times. Grasping at last that the call was for Maria, the woman dropped the receiver, and he could hear it clank like a hollow gourd against steel.

He told her he would meet her outside Lima Nights shortly before midnight. That would give her sufficient time to put in a good night's work and satisfy Jose Ferrari, and it would allow Bluhm to spend the evening with Fritz and Rudy, who had begged him to take them swimming at the Lima Cricket Club. She seemed happy to hear from him, warming at the prospect of a visit. But she was subdued, clearly circumspect. She said little other than "yes," "all right," "no." Just before she put down the phone, she added, "I miss you," and then she was gone.

The evening began with its distractions. On the way to the Cricket Club, Fritz and Rudy swore they could hear explosions coming from the direction of San Miguel, north, toward the airport, but it seemed little more than a disembodied rumble, hardly worth worrying about as they sped down Avenida Ejército, filled with joy. Like everyone else in that volatile city, Bluhm had learned to be careful. He never ventured far without listening to police reports on the radio. That afternoon, he had called the club ahead of time to be sure that security was good—that soldiers were where they should be around the property.

It had been at least a year since they'd been to the Cricket. The Bluhms were honorary members, granted that status in memory of Johann Bluhm, who had been one of the club's original trustees. When the boys were small, the family had made weekly outings there, but as time passed and the city slipped into belligerence, Sophie began to worry about the ride through those streets and found excuses not to go.

As the large white walls of the club loomed into view, Bluhm was reminded of his family's long history with the place: his grandparents' lavish parties in the ballroom, his father's impressive speeches at the Toastmasters Club, his own boyish attempts to swat red leather balls into the field's wickets. It all seemed so long ago—relics of a bygone era—until the guard waved the car through the gate and Bluhm crossed from slum to earthly heaven, prompting a brace of parking attendants in flawless white gloves to rush forward like annunciatory angels.

Bluhm settled into a comfortable rattan chair with a pencil and pad of paper and made out a little list of all the things he needed to do—wire Hamburg with an order for four Tessar lenses, wire Frankfurt for a separate order of three Wetzlars— but, before long, he was distracted by his sons. They caroused in the pool, racing each other for countless lengths, hurling themselves up in the air only to plunge back again, wriggling through the water like spirited dolphins at play. They were lean, well-muscled boys, with lambent eyes and happy faces, and it made Bluhm's heart swell to see them enjoy each other so fully. But as the evening wore on and they went from game to game, taking endless turns on the diving board, his mind began to be pulled by images that had plagued him for weeks. He began to study his watch and imagine where she might be at any given minute—in the supermarket, on a bus, at the bar—and all he could see was a perfect body spinning across the floor, catching light like a gossamer ribbon. He imagined her hair flared off one shoulder, whipping her face as she moved. He imagined her body in one of those split-second poses. The very thought of it stirred the want. He had tried to hold it back. It had been two full weeks since he had seen her.

By eleven-thirty he was parked across the street from the tango bar, doors locked, lights out. The place looked surprisingly boisterous for a Wednesday night, especially since it was days after Christmas, during that virginal week when people are shy to raise hell, having just praised the Lord. The tall black guard was turning revelers away, reminding them that the curfew would begin in little more than an hour. As the door opened and shut, he could see Jose Ferrari, two fists on the bar and grinning.

She came out the back, down the alley. Darting across the street, she seemed featherlight, buoyant, and, as she neared, he saw she was wearing the same pristine shirt she had worn a month ago, when they had sipped coffee in the little bakery in San Isidro. But this time her hair was pulled into two knots, one on either side of her face, and he was reminded of the dolls in pink and red that decorate the foyers of Chinese restaurants.

"It's me," he said, getting out of the car. She looked at him for a moment, not knowing what to expect, and then, silent, flew into his arms. She was smaller than he remembered, her brow no higher than his chest. He pressed his face into her hair and breathed in her scent: smoke and sugar. She was holding him fast—arms around his waist, forehead against his heart—as a daughter might hold her father. When she looked up, he could see himself in her eyes.

They drove a few blocks, laughing happily, before he realized that he had no idea where he was going. He had made no plans, imagined no setting beyond the confines of that vehicle. And, in any case, they didn't have much time, an hour at most before they would need to worry about the curfew. She didn't want food or drink, that much was clear from her hurried account of the evening: The dancers had had little to do but eat their allotted free bowls of rice and beans until the tables had begun to fill. After that, she had danced continuously for hours, so that her feet ached from the unforgiving prisons of her shoes. She took one of his hands from the wheel and pressed it to her ankle. "You feel how swollen I am?" she asked. But all he felt was desire, quick and hot as a new forged blade. It was all he could do to drive through San Borja calmly as she chattered on like a schoolgirl, squeezing his arm and flashing him mischievous little smiles until his hunger became unbearable.

"Take down your hair," he heard himself say as he stared ahead at the oncoming traffic. She paused to look at him but did as he asked, unwinding each knot carefully and fluffing out the hair so that it mounted her shoulders in thick black waves. "Good," he said. "Good." He could smell her fragrance more keenly now. It was fruit, always fruit, but there was something else tonight—a redolence more animal. Silk, maybe fur.

"Take off those pants." He couldn't help himself. It was wrong, sick. Part of him had said it, and another part was hearing it with alarm. He turned to look at her imperiously, lend his command some weight. But she met him with a look of approval. She unzipped, slid free of the garment, tossing the pants to her feet.

Her legs were like flickering screens under the passing streetlamps: glistening in the light; deep velvet in the shadow. A neat white V covered her pubis. He placed his hand on her knee and ran his fingers between her thighs until they touched the cotton. The skin was warm, firm, and, when he reached it, she rose up against the seat and gave a little gasp.

He pulled off Avenida Aviación and into a webwork of residential streets, looking for a dark alley. He found it by a tiny park that abutted the hospital grounds—it was a quiet street, hardly more than a block long, with modest houses. There were no guards, no lit windows. He switched off his headlights and coasted to a stop.

As soon as he cut the engine, she was on top of him. He slid back his seat to give her more room, but he hardly needed to. She was small and agile, and somehow she had managed to cast off the rest of her clothes and straddle him swiftly. Covering his face with kisses, his ears and neck with brisk little flicks of her tongue, she helped open his belt and zipper. He was fully aroused now, thrilled by her sureness of hand. There was nothing coy or shy in her—nothing that suggested the tenderness of her age. She was bold, carnal. Taking him eagerly into her hands, she guided him firmly toward her.

Their coupling was fierce, wordless—the only sound in that shroud of darkness the soft, fevered slap of their flesh. Only afterward, when she raised herself from him, did he see the smooth, perfect orbs of her breasts.

HE AWOKE THE NEXT MORNING with that image: her breasts emerging from the shadow, lifting from the plane of his chest. He rubbed his eyes and rolled over. His wife had already left the bed.

He showered, shaved, and went downstairs. He heard Sophie's light, musical laughter before he saw her. She was sitting at one end of the long white sofa in the living room, talking intently with the boys. The sun from the tall windows shone on the nape of her neck, and he could see that she had pinned up her hair. A few wayward strands hung down, as light as filament. Rudy was stretched out beside her, his head in her lap. Fritz was sprawled on a chair opposite them. They all looked clean, golden.

"How about Patricia?" Sophie was saying, as she ran her hands through Rudy's bright hair.

"Everyone wants to ask Patricia! She'd never go out with me!" Fritz wailed.

"Why ever not?" Sophie exclaimed.

"You haven't even tried!" Rudy added.

Bluhm headed to the kitchen for coffee. When he came back with a mug in hand, the conversation had moved on to another potential partner.

"We're talking about a school dance," Sophie said to her husband, and winked.

"So I gathered."

Rudy propped himself up on one elbow. "Pa! We've gone through every girl we can think of, and he keeps giving us excuses for why he can't ask any one of them!"

"Oh, Rudy," Fritz said with a sigh. "What do you know?"

"What do you mean what do I know?" Rudy asked, indignant.

"I mean, what do you know? You're such a child."

"Now, now," said Sophie.

"Does this young woman have to be a student at the university?" Bluhm ventured.

"No."

"Well, then. How about Willy's girl—Stephanie?"

Fritz looked at him, dumbfounded.

"What? You don't like her?" Bluhm said, surprised. "I think she's smart, pretty. You two always seem to get along!"

"Oh, Pa," Fritz said, with no little exasperation. "Stephanie's all right. I like her okay. But, for Chrissake, she's eighteen years old and still in high school! You think I want everyone laughing at me?"

Bluhm set down his coffee mug gently.

"That reminds me, Carlos," Sophie said—her memory, like his, turning to the night before. "Willy wasn't with you last night after you dropped off the boys, was he?"

Bluhm looked at her with his mouth open, uncertain what to say.

"Well? Was he?"

"No."

She pursed her lips and nodded.

"Why?"

"Oh, it's just that Beatriz called very late, after midnight. She was looking for Willy, beside herself with worry. I told her you said you were all going out to play cards, but you hadn't said where. And then suddenly I felt she suspected me as being part of it. You know. As if I were helping to cover up for him."

The boys exchanged knowing glances.

"I'm sure she didn't suspect anything of the kind," Bluhm said.

"Don't be so sure. If only Willy would make an effort to be more considerate to Beatriz! I think he's driving the poor woman crazy."

Bluhm couldn't look at his wife. He was no novice at

hiding his sins from her, but there was something else at work here, and he couldn't quite place it. A sharp pain shot through his head.

She went on. "Next time, maybe it would be a good idea to write down exactly where you're going."

"What good would that do? Didn't I just tell you that Willy wasn't with us?"

"You don't understand, do you, darling? I don't mean for Beatriz's sake. I mean for my own peace of mind."

IT WAS PREPOSTEROUS. Write down where he was going? Now? In this forty-fifth year of life? Never before had he felt it necessary to account for his comings and goings. Who did she think she was?

He had always had a firm rule: Never sleep twice with a quick conquest. It was a form of self-preservation—a prophylactic against messy involvements. But the next night he saw Maria again, if only to prove that he was not beholden to Sophie. Calling the house from an appointment downtown, he instructed Manuela to tell his wife he was delayed and wouldn't be home for dinner. He left no indication of where he would be. He picked up Maria in front of Lima Nights at ten and presented her with a large shopping bag from Ripley's. Inside were two summer dresses and a blouse.

Maria slipped into one of the dresses immediately, oblivious to people in passing cars who ogled her with astonishment. Bluhm kept turning to watch as she stripped to her

underwear, trying to keep a straight course as they sped mer-
rily down the Avenida Aviación. "Well?" she said, when she
was done. He was unprepared for the transformation. In the
light summer print, she seemed at once sensual and pure, like
a girl in a Gauguin painting.

He drove to a rotisserie place in Miraflores, where he
watched her savor a half chicken, ripping the cartilage from
the bone as if she hadn't eaten in days. After that, they made
long, slow love in an abandoned lot not far from the Parque
Kennedy. They ended with her cradled in his arms, the dress
hanging neatly from a hook in the backseat. As he kissed her
fingertips one by one, he could taste the chicken, and the unexpected flavor at once startled and touched him.

She was a child in every way but one. She had small
hands, small feet—toes that were more buds than flesh. She
had a child's fierce sense of truth. But she was a woman in the
act of love: her hunger so bold and unashamed, it took his
breath away.

"Where did you learn to make love like that?" he asked, as
they were dressing.

"From you."

He looked at her and smiled, but she was perfectly serious, her eyes gazing back at him evenly.

"And from the tango, of course," she added as an afterthought.

"Oh?"

"The way two people come together when they dance. To
me, it's just like life—a man and woman face each other;
he takes her hand. Then, suddenly, they're moving in perfect

harmony. They are one. And when it's over and the music stops, they walk away—two separate people again. Isn't that what sex is?"

"You are a philosopher," he said, brushing the hair from her face.

"I'm a dancer," she said, frowning. After a little while, she went on, "You know the tango 'Mano a Mano'?"

"My mother used to sing it all the time."

"It's my favorite. You know why?"

He shook his head.

"Because of how it ends."

"Tell me. I've forgotten."

"The two have gotten old. The love between them is long past. But there is still something there. Some little germ of feeling that will not die. I don't understand it. I don't know why. But it has always struck me as rare and beautiful."

He drew her face toward him in a kiss.

Before he put her on the bus to Lurigancho, they took pictures with one of his cameras. He showed her how it worked: the finder, the focus, the shutter. Posing for each other against the tan leather seats, they filled a whole roll, their flashes brightening the deep, starless night.

He found himself telling his friends all this a few nights later. He pulled the photographs from his breast pocket and showed them a Maria they didn't recognize. She was in a dress of crisp white cotton, its print littered with diminutive blue and yellow flowers. Bluhm had kissed off all her rouge, all her lipstick, and she looked like a perfectly innocent young girl—hair tucked behind the ears, legs pulled to one side, fingers around her bare toes.

Marco admitted he couldn't believe it was the same tart he had seen at Lima Nights—she looked, despite her race, altogether winning and wholesome. Willy tried hard to refrain from saying anything cruel but ended up blurting that he couldn't believe Bluhm was ravishing a child and then showing his friends the postcoital pictures. Oscar held on to the photographs for a long time, studying the ones of Bluhm more closely than the ones of Maria. When he was through, he handed them back, took off his glasses, and said very simply, "You look happy in those photographs, Carlos. I have to give you that."

Bluhm told them that his own feelings surprised him—the girl made him new again. It wasn't her age. He'd never been interested in females that age, and he didn't believe he'd be interested in any others. It was her boldness, her native intelligence, her unbridled sexual freedom.

"Boldness, intelligence, freedom—what a crock," said Marco. "It's power you like, my friend. She gives you the kind of power your wife or mine wouldn't know how to give a man."

"Not bad," said Oscar, half smiling. "Not bad, Doctor Marco. You deliver a fair analysis." But when he turned to Bluhm, his face became solemn again. "When you go home tonight, Carlos, I want you to think about a few things. I want you to consider very carefully what it is this child does for you. Think about each of the reasons you find her so irresistible, then ask yourself: Why? Why do you want this as much as you do? It's important for you to know exactly what you're doing."

Bluhm did exactly as he was told. After a pleasant dinner with Sophie, Dorotea, and the boys, he went into his study, sat in his father's comfortable chair, and contemplated the pleasures of Maria. There in the lamplight, in the company of his father's old books and pre-Columbian treasures, breathing the fragrant night air as it wafted through the open window, he began to reckon an inventory of his happiness. He began to attempt to understand his infatuation with the girl. He took a sheet of paper from the desk, drew a vertical line down the middle, and wrote out a brief list:

S.	M.
Day	*Night*
Domesticated	*Wild*
Headstrong	*Headstrong*
Obsessive	*Impulsive*
Good mother to her sons	*Good daughter to her mother*
Can wait	*Can't wait*
Hesitant in bed	*Curious i. b.*
Ashamed	*Unashamed*
Tuberoses	*Apples*
Dry	*Wet*

He stared at the sheet for a long time before the door opened and his mother's elfin face loomed in from the darkness. "You all right, Schätze?" she said, her eyes glimmering— even at that distance—like jewels.

"Yes, Mutti," he said. "I was just going over the accounts."

would be mistakes and he would be discharged like a stray into the brute sun. "Moron!" they'd yell as they pushed him out the door. Before long, he'd be back in Lurigancho, loitering around the empty lots.

He'd been mischievous as a boy—filching a sweet from a street vendor, a coin from a beggar's cup—but by the time he was thirteen, before that terrible night of the knife, his father had taught him well: Life is unkind, God can seem cruel, but if you are honest, work hard, stick by your family, you can survive this lousy world, get by. He and Pablito had done what they could to live by those simple mandates. Yes, Freddy was slow, Pablito quick to anger, and both incapable of the hard work prescribed. But they were harmless young men and, for all the bad luck, they had learned their father's first and third rules well: They did not lie. They stuck by family. And they were loyal to the mother fate had dealt them.

The next morning confirmed Freddy's apprehensions. Maria heard Berta Fernandez rise at dawn, as usual, and go out to begin her morning's work. But when she didn't hear the clatter of aluminum and the sounds of water rushing into the large wooden tub, she followed and found her mother squatting, holding an empty pail with trembling hands.

Why hadn't she noticed it before? Maria agonized. How had it escaped her that her own mother was so ill? She shook Pablito awake and begged him to get up, help with the laundry. Pablito grudgingly agreed. She quickly realized that she couldn't go off to San Isidro. How could she leave her family in such a state? They couldn't afford a doctor, and if some emergency were to happen, what would her brothers do?

4

Maria

SHE FOUND FREDDY ON THE STOOP, SMOKING A CIG-
arette, waiting to talk. He was worried about their mother.
Not about the drink or sex—intemperance they had long ac-
cepted. He wanted to talk about their mother's health. She
weighed too little, coughed too much. "Haven't you noticed?"
he said. "I think she's really sick this time. Dog sick. Ever
since her last brawl with that jackass."

Maria studied her brother. He had a wide, friendly face
and gentle black eyes, and for all the privations of hunger they
had suffered together in childhood, he was hale and muscular.
He had big shoulders, strong hands. But those hands seldom
found steady work on the fickle streets of Lima. He would labor for a while in construction, or as a meatpacker, or rotting
his nails plucking chickens in poultry vats, but he couldn't
hold down a job. It was a slight slowness of mind, an inability
to think on his feet. Days would go by, maybe a week, and he
might be given the benefit of the doubt. But eventually there

They had no money for a clinic. She called the supermarket to explain it all to fat Robertito, but the number only rang and rang. Eventually she gave up; there was so much to do, and she was only wasting valuable time. She took off her blouse and skirt, put on an old shift, and headed out to do the wash.

Morning had brought five or six men, dropping off dirty bundles of prison uniforms, but by noon the doorway was a hive of angry women, demanding clean clothes. Some of the garments were ready. Most were not—hanging on lines, unironed, or on the cement floor in the same grimy wads people had tossed there the day before. Maria promised that all would be ready by nightfall.

Had the gash to her mother's head done this? The lover who had inflicted it was long gone—no more than a fleeting memory—but Maria understood now that his fists had left an indelible mark on Berta Fernandez. Her very nature seemed changed: She was no longer funny, no longer agile. While they bustled about—scrubbing, rinsing, ironing the damp clothes dry—she sat in a corner with her glass of fermented chicha, coughing too much and eyeing her children sourly. She seemed shriveled and far away, a husk of her former self. But with the close of day and the customers come and gone, they managed to take her inside and feed her a good meal of corn and potatoes. At that point, sitting across the rickety table from her frail mother and exhausted brothers, Maria decided to tell them about Bluhm.

They listened in awe as she spoke of the big house in San Isidro. She told them of the shiny black car and how it had come for her at Lima Nights; how she had cruised in it through the streets of the capital; how it had transported her to the park and the chicken rotisserie place. She brought out the dresses and held each in front of her, letting them touch the fabric, feel the worth. She showed them the black collar with the silver heart. She described the particulars of Bluhm's face, his genial blue eyes, the receding gold hair—guessing his age at about forty. She told of his neatly ironed shirts, his fancy watch, his cameras, his habit of leaning in close when he wanted to make a point.

Berta Fernandez eyed her daughter warily and, when she was finished, said simply, "A man with so many possessions must have a wife too."

"Yes. And children. But that doesn't make him a happy man."

"I know this guy!" Freddy said. "I think I've seen that big black car driving around here."

"Don't be an idiot," said Pablito. "Nobody comes to Lurigancho with a car like that unless it's some government goon, counting the jailbirds."

"So, what does this mean?" said their mother, pushing away her empty plate and planting her elbows on the table. "Where are you going with this pretty little story?"

"I think he's in love with me."

"Ha!" her mother croaked. "One dip in your sweet little pie and he'll be off, fast as he can, back to his wife and children. What do men ever want?"

"No! He keeps coming—"

"You want to play that game, Maria? Fine," the decrepit woman said with as much vigor as she could summon. "Who am I to stop you? I play my little games; you play yours. You think that the great Señor Bluhm is going to whisk you off and give you the good life? He'll give you a belly, that's what. Forget the big house and car. You'll be stuck with a kid in your gut. Maybe he'll acknowledge the brat, maybe he won't. If he gives you money, congratulations, you win the lottery. If he doesn't, there you'll be, flat on your back, with a baby to feed." Berta Fernandez was suddenly gripped by a frenzy of coughing. She clutched her shirt and hung on for dear life. But she had more to say. "You remember Nora?" she gasped. "That girl down the road who kept having the babies? She was a maid in a rich man's house. You take one good look at those curly-haired snot noses and tell me they don't have a rich white father. Did the sonofabitch give her anything? Not on your life!"

Maria shifted in her chair, amazed to hear her mother—as profligate as she was—arguing for caution.

"Are you in love with this man?" asked Freddy.

She turned to look at her brother's big, open face. "I think he's nice ... He seems to care ... I like ..." But she stopped, hearing the sound of her own indecision. "I don't know what love is," she said finally.

"Love!" Pablito said, leaning back in his chair with a grin. "Everyone knows what love is."

"Oh, shut up!" his mother shouted. "No one's in love here!" In time, she asked, "So, what do you want from Carlos Bluhm?"

"What do I want?" Maria couldn't believe the absurdity of the question. Didn't her mother understand that more than anything she wanted to get out? She spread her hands on the table and spoke slowly. "Are you asking me if I want to spend my life with Carlos Bluhm? Are you asking me if I want to be safe—live in that house, sit in that garden, lie in his bed?" Maria drummed her fingers on the worm-chewed wood, weighing the evidence of her wretched circumstances. Her mother was gaunt, her face a cathedral of bones. Freddy was staring at her with an open mouth, his pink tongue thick between his teeth. Only Pablito seemed to have anything resembling an alert look on his face, and he brought it toward her slowly, across the table. "Go on, Maria. Don't stop. You want all those nice things for yourself?"

"Yes. I do. Of course I do." And then she added in a whisper, "I just want to feel safe. That's all."

"And so do we, pretty baby. So do we."

BLUHM CALLED two days later. His friend Marco would get them a room in his hotel, he said, but Marco was all business. He'd been quick to lay out the rules: They could stay no more than one hour. He didn't want them in the way of paying customers. They had to arrive at eleven in the morning and stay no later than twelve, when the staff would begin making its rounds, tidying the rooms.

This meant that for the second time that week she would be making excuses to Fat Robertito. The manager had been surly about the day she'd missed, saying he'd had to go to lengths to find a replacement, even pitch in himself. But she calculated that if she got to work by twelve-thirty, she could sweet-talk her way into his good graces.

There was another calculus at work. She was determined to win Bluhm, hold on as long as she could. She had no experience in this. She felt she was stumbling in the dark, entering a world she could never know, feeling her way through his heart like a blind woman in a maze. But if she could make him reliant on her, as Monica at Lima Nights assured her she could—if she became his mistress—there would be little use for Fat Robertito or the slick-haired Jose. She wouldn't need those jobs at all. And so, as a good gambler decides what cards should stay and what cards can move, she began placing all bets on the camera salesman.

The moment they walked into the room on the ninth floor of the Cesar Hotel, it was clear how Marco had been able to manage it. He had given Bluhm a room whose guests had checked out minutes before. It was littered with towels, the air redolent with soap and steam. There were empty bottles of Cusqueña beer, crumpled wrappers of fast food, a coffeemaker that was half full, still on. The bedclothes were rumpled at the foot of the bed, and six pillows were stacked on a chair—leaving the bed free of encumbrances.

She had never seen anything like it—the grandness, the palatial luxury—but she also sensed there was something wrong too: in the disorder of the room, in the love to be seized so quickly. She had little time to contemplate it. Bluhm's eagerness was palpable. As quickly as he took measure of the mayhem, he dismissed it. She was setting out her lucky amulets, lining them up on the bureau, when Bluhm pulled her into his arms and kissed her deeply. She moved quickly to accommodate him, unbuttoning her blouse, and suddenly his lips were on her neck, the base of her throat, her shoulders, her breasts. Lifting her up, he set her on the bed and undressed the rest of her, studying her nakedness in the gauzy light, running his fingers over her pubis as if it were a precious stone.

With infinite patience he traced every inch of her, tasting her nipples, her navel, her groin, her thighs, until he reached the wet heart of her cut. He took her at last on the edge of the bed, on his knees, and after he was done, he pulled her down to the floor and into his arms. They lay for a long while like that, limbs entwined, listening to each other's breath, the muffled voices in the hall, the cries of vendors outside, the incessant rumble of traffic as it sped those with greater cares up and down the busy avenue.

"Oscar told me I should beware of falling in love with a child," he said. "But I don't think of you that way. To me, you're a woman. Every bit my equal."

"Who's Oscar?" she said, raising herself up on one elbow.

"My friend, the psychiatrist."

She looked at him blankly.

"A little like your fortune-teller," he said, laughing. "He reads dreams and minds and then tells you what to expect if you don't do as he says. Of course, he never talks about anything as interesting as swallowing sharks, but now and then he may give you a glimpse into someone's head. People are willing to pay him good money for that."

"Does he use lucky charms?"

"No, darling," he said. "No charms, no amulets. A swinging pendant, a bit of hypnotism—that's as mystical as it gets. And blotches of ink that reveal your state of mind. But no prayers or lucky beads. Nothing like that."

She took his big hands and stroked their fingers. They were pale, strong, with patches of gold hair on the knuckles. She imagined them on the steering wheel of his car or wrapped around a camera. Or reaching for the familiar comforts of his wife. Maria started, her grip on his flesh deepening. She wanted desperately to ask what kind of woman shared his bed every night—what skill, what charm had put her there in the first place. But she held her tongue.

"Do you remember, Señor Bluhm, when you and I sat in the pastry shop and you told me I had to watch out for bad men? That they would take what they wanted and throw what was left to the hills of Lurigancho?"

He nodded yes.

"You wouldn't do that to me, would you? You wouldn't discard me like an old rag?" She felt a sharp twinge in her stomach as she said it. It was a question she had asked herself often in the last few days, now that her mother had prompted it. When would he leave her? When would he get enough and move on? She felt his heart beating steadily under her face.

"No, of course not. I would never do that to you," he said gently. She looked up, met his gaze, and realized it was true. Comforted, she nestled back into his arms.

They talked in lazy circles after that, agreeing on some things they both loved: the color yellow, the warmth of the sun, the smell of the ocean. She had never been on a beach, had only seen one from the green cliffs of Miraflores—but she had admired the roadside billboards with their images of near-naked lovers under wide umbrellas. It was, she confessed, her idea of heaven.

A shrill ringing tore them from their reveries. Marco was on the telephone, telling them it was over. He would be waiting for them downstairs.

She was still pulling the knots from her hair when they walked off the elevator into the lobby. Bluhm's friend stood by the cluster of ornately carved chairs by the main entrance, watching the armed guards outside. For as handsome and affable a man as Bluhm had described—and as she dimly remembered—he seemed stiff and dour. He barely acknowledged her presence except to make a quick survey of her body as she approached. Bluhm gave him the room key, palming it deftly into his hand. The hotel manager didn't return Bluhm's smile. He slapped Bluhm on the back and fairly shouted, "Bring a whiter one next time, Carlos, and I'll throw in some free champagne."

FAT ROBERTITO WAS FLYING from one cash register to the next, a cluster of keys in his hand. She tried to slip past and change into her uniform quickly, but he caught sight of her just as she was turning the corner into the dry-goods aisle. He shouted her name and pointed sharply toward the office.

"Thunderbolt!" a coworker whispered as she hurried past.

Santa Isabel was making one of its "lightning inspections." She had heard of these—the supermarket was famous for them—but she hadn't worked there long enough to experience one. When she stepped into the stuffy little office, the sight of a tall, red-haired stranger standing over the harried accountant confirmed it. He looked on imperiously while the nervous little man punched numbers into a machine. As soon as he saw her, he motioned her in. He had a lilting quality to his speech, and it took her a moment to realize that he, like the ownership of the supermarket, was Chilean. She gave him a solicitous smile, but he drew himself up to his full height and appraised her sternly, unfazed by the pretty face. "We've been waiting for you, Maria Fernandez."

She tried to issue an apology, but he ignored it and his next words came unheralded. "Let me put it as directly as I can. This company is an ark of efficiency. We pride ourselves on it. We do not tolerate tardiness. We take truancy as an affront. In my country your behavior would be unacceptable, and it is unacceptable here, on this little patch of Chilean ground. We are trying to teach our staffs a sense of accountability, something it appears you don't have, señorita. Your attendance records indicate that you have been delinquent more than once, coming late, leaving early—sometimes not bothering to show up at all. We will not have it. I'm letting you go."

"No!" She felt the blood race to her ears. She had expected to be reprimanded, penalized, humiliated. But not this. "Please. I can explain all of it. I tried to call—"

He put a large, freckled hand into the air and shook his head. "Don't waste your time, señorita. And please don't waste mine. The books show we owe you no pay. On the contrary, you owe us a day's labor. Go now, and I won't ask you to refund that money. We'll consider it even. Good-bye." He leaned down and rapped his big knuckles on the desk, prompting the accountant to close his mouth and continue with his sums.

Maria reeled through the aisles, her face red with the rebuke. Deaf to her coworkers' whispers, she made her way to the door and out into the brute afternoon sun. She had nowhere to go, no notion of what to do. Her instinct was to call Bluhm, but he had always been so strict about the rules: She was never to telephone him at home. And home was where he surely was, at work in his study. Absently, she wandered down the avenue toward a park. It was barely one-thirty; she wouldn't be needed at Lima Nights for another five hours. She followed the winding footpaths around and around until, dazed and exhausted, she slumped onto a bench and wept.

For more than an hour, she replayed the foreigner's cruel words, wiping away hot tears in a cycle of fury and regret. The man had described a person she didn't recognize: a laggard, a truant, a thief. Eventually, fatigue overcame her and she slept. When she awoke, children were playing on the grass, shouting and throwing pebbles at one another. Their laughter made her feel even more wretched. Worse still were the lovers, strolling arm in arm, pressing themselves hungrily into each other. Seeing them, she decided to ignore caution.

At a nearby public telephone she dialed his house. An elderly woman answered. Who could that possibly be? As calmly as she could, she asked for Señor Bluhm, but even the sound of her own voice seemed alien—it was thick, verging on tears, impossible to control.

"I don't understand you, señorita. Would you please speak more clearly? You want Señor or Señora Bluhm? And which Señora Bluhm, if it's the latter? There are two of us here, my dear."

Maria's chin began to quiver. "Carlos! Carlos Bluhm!" she shouted.

There was a brief silence and then, "Who's calling?"

"Señorita Fernandez." She added, "From Santa Isabel."

There was a muffled sound, as if the old woman were trying to put a hand over the receiver, but Maria could hear her say, "Sophie, is Carlos here? Someone from the supermarket wants to speak with him."

"Who is it?" The other voice was brisk, clear, as if it were right there, in the same room.

"Señorita Fernandez from the market."

"No, Mutti. He's not here. He said he'd be on calls all day today. Can you take a message? What could they possibly want with him?"

"Oh, I bet I know who that is," a young man's voice said brightly. He was close by too, together with the women. "It's that friend of his. That girl at the checkout. The one who works two jobs."

"What girl . . . ?" but the words were muffled as the old lady fumbled with the phone.

"Señorita," she said at last, "is it something I can help you with? Some information perhaps? Or would you care to leave your name and number?"

Maria felt the sharp prick of desperation. There were so many voices on the other end. So many people between her and Bluhm: Two women who claimed his name. A son. There was a full, human life pulsing in that house, a universe far greater than the one she shared with him. She had always suspected it might be so but hadn't allowed herself to consider it—her only goal the warm refuge of his arms.

She hung up the phone and walked through the streets of San Isidro, clutching her bag to her chest. There were elegant shop windows, flea-bitten beggars, flirtatious laborers—all eager for her attention—but she was too numb to pay them any mind. Eventually she crossed the bridge over the roaring Paseo de la República, aiming as best she could for the streets of San Borja. It was a long journey and she lost her way more than once, but by four-thirty in the afternoon she reached the Avenida Aviación. Lima Nights was closed, the service door shut and bolted with a giant padlock. She pounded on the front door, and suddenly the little rectangular slat slid open and she saw Jose Ferrari's lizard face. His tiny eyes widened when he realized who it was. He opened the door, amazed.

"Jesus God, woman," he said. "What happened? You look like the back end of hell."

. . .

BLUHM WAS FURIOUS. How had she dared call him at home, identify herself by her real name, disclose her place of work? Sophie was out on the patio cutting Dorotea's hair when she told him. It was near sunset; he had walked out with a glass of cold beer in hand and was listening to his wife describe the beach house she'd found for them in Paracas. "A cottage with a full kitchen," Sophie was saying excitedly, "only a few blocks from a fruit and vegetable market!" when suddenly she remembered the call from Santa Isabel. She whirled around with the scissors in her hand, its blades pointing straight to his heart. "Someone from the supermarket was trying to reach you, Carlos," she said.

"Señorita Fernandez," Dorotea added with simple certitude. The old woman turned stiffly in her chair and peered over her glasses. "I've always thought that the help in that supermarket was well trained and polite, but this girl was rude. She didn't talk; she shouted. And then when I asked whether she wanted to leave a message, she just hung up!"

"Was it Juana Maria Fernandez?" Manuela asked calmly. "If so, she's called here before." She was sweeping the wisps of gray hair into a dustpan, dropping them onto the dirt behind the verbena.

"Really?" Sophie said. "Did she tell you why she was calling?"

"She said she was looking for Fritz," the maid answered. "I thought she was one of his friends. This was several weeks ago, Señora. But she hung up on me too; maybe that's why I remember it now."

"I can't imagine that any of Fritz's friends would work at a supermarket," Dorotea said. "And, in any case, he was right there in the living room when she called." She fixed her piercing blue eyes on her son. "If I remember correctly, dear, Fritz said you knew her."

Bluhm's head spun with the gyre of possible excuses. "Well, well, ladies," he said as steadily as he could manage. "You've gone and ruined my surprise."

"Surprise?" Sophie said brightly.

"Yes. A special order." He stopped there, not for effect. He needed more time to think it through. But the lie needed no further embellishment. "That's all the information you get," he said.

Dorotea clapped her hands, and hair tumbled from her shoulders like down from a preening bird. "A surprise!" she sang, delighted. He nodded at her, smiling.

The fury came later.

After dinner, he got in the car and sped out into the night. How could she have done that to him? How could she have been so reckless?

She was where he knew she would be: out on the dance floor, in a wheelwork of busy motion. Alone in a crowd of men, he watched her. She was wearing the black and red costume she'd worn on the first night he'd seen her. He remembered her walking up boldly in that dress, offering him her hand. So much had happened since: He had held her in his arms, possessed her, felt her warmth, tasted her salt. He retreated to the bar, sobered now. But Maria went on, moving spiritedly to the music. She rose to her toes and flung herself back, her spine arched over her partner's arm. And yet, for all that energy, her expression was lifeless—for a fleeting instant he wondered if he was looking at someone else's face.

He put an elbow on the bar to steady himself. The place was sweltering, smoke clouding the air, blurring the edges of everything around him. Someone had thrown open a door and curling in from the street came the unmistakable stench of urine. Bluhm glanced about at the chance congregation of revelers, many of them ordinary men out on the town, looking to forget, brought there by failure and heartache. The large tables were noisy and boisterous, the work of forgetting multiplied many times. The small tables were filled with couples holding hands, their faces illuminated by candlelight. Bluhm pulled out a stool, called to the bartender, and ordered a glass of whiskey.

The liquor quickly relaxed him. What was the point of making a scene? In good time he'd give her a scolding. For the moment it felt right to sit, stare openly at strangers, wonder what coils of mortality had brought them together. He let his eyes roam the darkness, alighting on one couple, then another, until they fell on two lovers at the far end of the room. The man had his back to him: He was almost bald, with a thick neck and broad shoulders. He leaned over the table, holding the woman's plump wrist with two hands, kissing her fingers as she talked animatedly. She was clearly pleased. She smiled broadly, tilting her head like a coquette with a gesture that was oddly familiar until Bluhm realized he was looking at Carmela. And that was Willy, chattering at her side.

Bluhm took his drink and pressed through the crowd

toward them. They were delighted to see him. Willy pulled up an extra chair, slapped Bluhm on the back. The two men shared pleasantries and, to Bluhm's surprise, Carmela seemed uncharacteristically gracious. She smoked her cigarette and listened quietly, smiling blissfully at his friend. After a while, Willy could contain himself no longer. "Bluhm," he said, "take a good look at Carmela. See anything new?" Bluhm saw it immediately—a large topaz, glittering from her left hand. But no sooner did he open his mouth to comment than a breathless voice came from behind. "Can we talk?"

He turned and saw Maria.

"I need to talk to you now, Carlos. Alone."

"You need to talk to everyone, it seems," he said coldly. "Including every last person in my house."

She stood still for a moment, speechless. And then she blurted, "I was fired from Santa Isabel today!"

Her mouth was trembling. She was suddenly, indisputably a child: painted, trussed, tricked out in satin and ruffles, but a helpless child all the same. So, she had left their hotel room and gone from joy to catastrophe. It all made sense now—the desperate call, the failure of judgment. He reached out and took her hand.

Willy glanced at Carmela's startled face and signaled with a nod that this was the girl he had told her about in earlier conversation. Carmela did not hesitate. She leaned in and stroked the little dancer on the arm. "Oh, poor doll! You lost your job? That's a terrible thing, honey." She grabbed a chair and pointed to the seat, urging the girl to sit beside her.

Carmela seemed the perfect antidote for Maria's troubles.

Armed with a gaudy new ring, she sprang to cheer her with friendly babble. She told Maria about the many times she'd been fired by her employers—starting with the insurance company where she'd met her beloved Willy. And the funny thing was: Every time she got fired, something better seemed to come her way.

Maria was heartened by those stories, and soon they were ordering drinks all around. Jose Ferrari himself brought a platter of grilled anticuchos to their table. As they dove into the meat hungrily, Carmela told Maria that her big goal, in fact, was to be fired from her current job. She was weary of working in that luggage shop, hearing the rich boast about where they were going on vacation—she needed a vacation herself!

They all laughed at that.

"So, where would you go, Carmela, with so much world at your disposal?" Bluhm asked.

"The world?" she said. "I don't need a whole world, Bluhm. I just want Willy to take me down the coast to Punta Hermosa or Pucusana."

"The beach!" Maria cried. "I've never been. What a wonderful idea!"

"Well, of course you've never been," Carmela said with a wink. "You can't very well be sunning your fanny if you're here, slaving away in this dump, can you? I think I'll work at that shop for another month or so, just long enough to get a discount on a nice set of suitcases. Then I'll *insist* that this handsome man of mine sweep me off to a nice white beach and a good fish dinner."

Willy squeezed her hand. "There's a beach right here,

sweetest love. And good restaurants with umbrellas where you can sit out and eat fish so fresh it jumps into your pretty little mouth."

"Ceviche!" Carmela squealed. "How I love it! But, darling, I have my heart set on eating a good plate of it on a *real* beach, far away from these noisy streets! Everyone who comes into our store says there's no comparison: The city beaches are filthy; the ones in the south, though, are heaven."

Bluhm was struck by the woman's sense of entitlement. Wasn't it enough that his friend paid her rent? Willy was not a wealthy man, but he was flinging a good portion of his salary her way—risking his family's welfare in the process. And the ring she was waving so flamboyantly in their faces: How had he managed to buy that? For all her solicitude tonight, she was the same greedy parasite she'd ever been. How much more did she think she could squeeze out of Willy? This carnival couldn't go on forever. The music was bound to stop.

"Do you hear that, Carlos?" Maria whispered. She was tugging at his sleeve, her black eyes glowing. "He's taking her to the beach! Can we do that too? Can you and I go down the coast, just the two of us? For a few days?"

5

Carlos

THE MORE SOPHIE TALKED ABOUT THE HOUSE IN Paracas, the more Bluhm wished he were going there with Maria. The idea came to him one morning, curled into his brain, and grew.

Making love in his car had become, for all practical purposes, untenable. Especially in past weeks when car bombs had destroyed three government offices and soldiers were patrolling every block. Even an empty office, when he could arrange it, was a vexing prospect. There was always the feeling that someone could barge in—that the act of sex, by necessity, had to be clumsy and rushed. The prospect of ten full days— walking together openly on the warm sand, holding Maria all night long, swimming nude at daybreak—began to seem the realization of all desire.

There was, too, a discernible change in Sophie. She had begun to nag him about household finances. It hadn't taken long for her to notice that Bluhm was spending more money—money they didn't have. He had made excuses, torn up the receipts for all the clothes he had bought Maria. But there were more clothes after that, and more gifts, not to mention lunches now that Maria was free during the day. Sophie began to watch his expenses more closely and to complain. There was nothing less agreeable than her face across the table on a day when she reckoned accounts.

So it followed that when a full turkey buffet for eight, complete with cake, ice cream, and candles, was delivered from Santa Isabel supermarket for Rudy's seventeenth birthday—a surprise Bluhm was absolutely obliged to execute—Sophie was so angry she could barely speak. She remained tight-lipped through dinner, keeping her own counsel as her husband and mother-in-law chatted on about the old days and Rudy and Fritz served themselves seconds of everything and went off happily to their rooms. But later, when Bluhm emerged from the bathroom in his pajamas, she was waiting for him: standing in the middle of the bedroom with her jaw rigid as a clamp. "So that was the surprise you've been planning?" she asked. "The upshot of all those mysterious calls from Santa Isabel?"

"Yes. I think he liked it. Don't you?"

"I think he might have preferred a real gift from his father. He was just being polite. Don't you know your own son, Carlos?"

"Oh, stop, Sophie. It was fine."

"It was not fine. I don't think you understand what's fine anymore. How much did you spend on all that food? It wasn't better than any dinner Manuela might have made! And now most of it will go to waste. What's gotten into you?"

He couldn't very well tell her the truth: that he had needed to make a lie good; that he had needed to buy a reason for his lover's imprudent telephone calls. "Okay. It was a bad idea," he said, and, to erase the glowering look on her face, switched off the bedroom lights.

There was more. He hadn't made love to Sophie in months. At first, to allay suspicions, he had performed his husbandly charge. Done it admirably. Sex with his wife had never been difficult when he was straying with women he didn't know. There was never a face to summon. But ever since he had made love to Maria, he was crawling into bed with her perfect little face in mind. And so the prospect of going to Paracas with a carping wife, his elderly mother, and two teenage boys—the thought of being without his lover for ten full days—seemed, with every passing hour, a penance. Pondering it in his father's old chair one Sunday afternoon, he reached into the desk, drew out the list that compared his wife to his lover, crossed out the *Hesitant* before *in bed* and wrote over it in square black letters *NULL*. It was a silly thing to do, impossibly childish, but it was salve for the moment, remedy for the gall.

He was slumped there, contemplating these things, when his son began to play *"Erbarme Dich"* in the other room. It began with its plaintive melody, building slowly, the grace notes forging a complicated cadence until the prayer soared from his father's instrument with a rapture he had not heard before.

Bluhm knew every note of that piece by heart, could sense the virtuosity of this performance. The force of that comprehension, the joy of hearing Rudy's hands move fearlessly over his father's cello, brought a sharp burn to his eyes. If only the old man could have lived to hear it. Here was grace for a man's imperfections, salve for his human failings—balm for the soul indeed.

He found Rudy locking the cello into its great black case and sliding it into its place under the piano. Bluhm sat on the sofa and crossed his feet on the elaborately carved coffee table. "Son, every time you play that, it gets better. I think you've surpassed your grandfather by now. He'd be so proud."

"I play it for you, Pa. I know it pleases you." Rudy seemed exhilarated as he brushed the hair from his face, his forehead dappled with perspiration. Bluhm marveled at the physical effort it took to produce such ethereal sound.

"It does please me," he said. "Very much."

The boy sat across from him and grinned. "Enough to let me go over to Sebastian's this afternoon?" He raised a foot and tapped his father's shoe playfully. "It's kind of boring around here today."

"Sure. As long as you're not out on the streets. But check with your mother first."

"Thanks."

"Are you looking forward to the beach, Rudy?" Bluhm asked after a moment.

His son shrugged.

"What does that mean?"

"Mom's excited about it. Grandma's not. If you want to

know the truth, Fritz and I would rather stay in town. We don't know anyone in Paracas! Our friends are all here."

The words pulled Bluhm up. "Are you serious?"

"I don't want to sound ungrateful! But you ask and I want to be honest. It's just that Fritz and I will miss our friends, you know? Sebastian has invited me to his house up the coast later this summer and I'd really like to go. His cousins are all my age . . ."

Could it be that the only one who really wanted to go on this godforsaken pilgrimage was Sophie? The thought tripped into another. And then something turned in Bluhm's brain.

". . . I really don't want to stir up trouble, Pa, but I'd much rather spend that week with Sebastian. You asked me for the truth. There it is."

"Thanks, Rudy. I appreciate your candor. No offense taken whatsoever." The boy sat back, relieved. "Now let me ask you another question," his father added. "But again, you have to tell me the absolute truth."

"Sure. Ask away."

"How did you like your birthday dinner?"

"You want the honest-to-God truth?"

His father nodded.

"I loved it, Pa. It was so nice of you to do that for me. I thought it was just grand."

IT TOOK BLUHM A FULL DAY to think it through, another day to accustom himself to the idea, and on the third day, as a brisk, purging wind swept in from the Pacific and carried away every trace of early-morning fog, he screwed tight his courage and went looking for his wife.

Sophie was out on the veranda, fluffing her freshly shampooed hair and reading *Who Killed Palomino Molero?*, a new novel by Vargas Llosa. She was dressed in a crisp white piqué shift and, with both legs tucked under her, she looked as aloof and inaccessible as a stone nymph.

He asked about the book. She looked up as if she were returning from a great distance. It was about a young soldier, she explained, a handsome Indian recruit found murdered near his air force base. The detective suspects him of having had a secret love affair with the commanding officer's daughter—a white woman.

He nodded, then pushed ahead quickly, noting the unexpected correspondence, afraid of losing his nerve. "I have bad news."

"What is it?" Her eyes grew dark; she leaned forward.

"We have to cancel our trip to Paracas."

"Whatever for?"

"I just got off the phone with Zeiss. My boss wants me to come to Germany that week."

"Oh, Carlos! No!"

"I'm sorry, darling. Sorrier than I can say."

"But I've put a deposit on the place! And it's not refundable!"

"I understand. Why don't you give me the agents' telephone number? I'll call and try to convince them to give back our money. It's long enough away and high season—I'm sure there are others who would love to rent that place. In any case, I've created this mess, so I should be the one to get us out of it."

"I'd be amazed if they listen to you," she said. "It's a long-standing rule with them. Oh, darling, this is the worst news. I was looking forward to it so much!" He felt a quick stab of guilt, but it was hardly enough to stop him.

"I know, I know. But there's absolutely nothing I can do. You understand, don't you? Give me the information. I'll get that refund and see if they can accommodate us some other time."

He followed her to the nook between foyer and living room, to the tiny, inlaid Florentine writing desk that had once belonged to his grandmother. From one of its cubbyholes she pulled a long, cream-colored envelope. Inside was a letter confirming the rental. He took it, kissed her on the forehead, and retreated quickly to his study.

It didn't take long to arrange things with the agency. He explained that there was a change in family plans and that all communication should be directed to him in the future. He arranged to come by their Lima office the next day with the full payment in hand.

Already, he could feel the sand underfoot, smell the subtle perfume of the Huacachina flower, sense the joy of having Maria however and whenever he wanted her. Never in his life had anticipation been so acute—even as a young man, contemplating the consummation of his marriage, and certainly never with any of his passing assignations. It was as if it had taken him forty-four years to ripen to this point, forty-four years to reach a stage at which every fiber of his being awaited the pleasure such an interlude might bring.

He told Sophie he would take advantage of his time in Germany by submitting the old Peugeot for a long-needed trip to the mechanic. When she worried about the cost, he assured her he would squeeze an incentive bonus from the company. Didn't he make use of that car in every one of his sales trips?

It was all Fritz and Rudy could do to keep from cheering the news openly. They quickly secured permission for time on the beach with their friends' families. Dorotea winked at them conspiratorially and downed a full glass of schnapps.

The next morning, Bluhm took two of his father's most precious ceramics from the pre-Columbian collection in the study, wrapped them carefully in old copies of *El Comercio*, and ferried them away to a gloomy apartment above an antiques shop on Conquistadores. There he negotiated to sell them for more than the amount of money he needed for the beach house, plus an amount equivalent to Sophie's deposit. Pocketing the cash, he drove directly to the rental office in downtown Lima. And so, by early afternoon, having executed those transactions, he swung his car east and headed triumphantly for the hills of Lurigancho.

He had never been there before, but with a good map he was able to determine the route easily. Other than the fact that there was a prison, he knew little about the place. He recalled the news coverage some months before of a terrorist uprising that had culminated in the brutal execution of hundreds of inmates. In truth, he hadn't paid much mind. It had seemed so far away. And, in any case, it had all taken place within the confines of the prison's walls.

He turned off the main highway to Avenida 9 Octubre and drove slowly along the district's main artery, registering the rows of unsightly warehouses and crumbling adobe. *Kill the rich capitalist pigs!* was scrawled in angry black paint across one storefront. *Now!* an adjoining wall answered. A gold star on a red field was festooned with the name *Mao*. A blackened pylon, burned by a crude bomb, jutted from the dirt, its wires dangling. There were no proper houses, no shops—only endless shacks with corrugated metal roofs that rose up into the hills in a hundred directions.

After a short while he saw the jail in the distance. Maria had said something about its proximity to her house. How many laundries could there possibly be in a neighborhood, anyway? But as the car struggled up the dirt road toward that stronghold, he was hardly able to see: The road was full of ruts and rocks, and a suffocating gray dust billowed from beneath his wheels, invading his senses. He rolled up his window and wiped his face with his sleeve, leaving a damp streak of brown. When he looked up, he saw two women loom out of the haze, laboring under dingy buckets of water. He wrenched his steering wheel sharply to the left and the car snaked around them. They turned to watch him pass.

Rubble was everywhere, strewn in the streets and piled high in empty lots, hoarded for some unknown purpose. Empty plastic rolled aimlessly in a capricious wind. Seeing a cluster of sullen young men on a corner, Bluhm stopped against all better judgment and asked to be directed to the house of Maria Fernandez, but they only stared back with hostile eyes. When he repeated the question, adding that her mother ran a laundry, a boy with a pockmarked face ambled up, put his elbows on the roof, and leaned in to gawk at the dashboard, a rancid stink in his hair. No, the youth replied tersely, he'd never heard the name, but as he said it, he snapped the fingers of one hand. His companions walked slowly toward them. Bluhm felt his stomach lurch. He rolled up the glass, and the boy's arms flew up and off the car defensively; then Bluhm locked all the doors, slammed the engine in gear, and drove on.

He understood now what a foolish expedition he'd made. In all the excitement of procuring the beach house, he thought he could find Maria easily, surprise her with the news. He had not imagined it would be this complicated. This frightening. He hadn't imagined this was how she lived.

He pulled the car over, wheeled around, tried to retrace his course. As he picked up speed, dust spat from his wheels, then curled in a sinister tail behind him. He could see the main road below, down the hill. He was moving quickly now, bouncing so vigorously that his teeth clacked in his head. Suddenly he heard sharp little bursts of sound, as if the rocks that littered the road were flying up and striking the flanks of his car. He glanced at the side mirror to confirm it but saw instead a group of seven or eight children running behind, throwing stones. They were laughing, but their faces were full of malice. And they were shouting so clearly, there was no mistaking their words: "Vampire! Bloodsucker!" they screeched. "Get away! Go!"

. . .

THE IMAGES CAME BACK in dreams: the children's forbidding laughter, the pockmarked face, the women struggling under the pails, the sudden battery of stones. It took him days to forget them.

He never mentioned it to Maria. It was hard enough to square the beauty of the girl with the loathsomeness of her place; he feared he might betray the depth of his disgust. He forced himself to think only of her eyes, the fresh apple of her hair, the burnt nutmeg of her skin, the sweet, spontaneous happiness in her voice when she learned that a house awaited her in Paracas. As days passed, they went together to buy the things she would need: a pair of sandals, a swimsuit, sunglasses, halter tops, frilly lingerie, a brightly striped bag to hold it all. Her joy was catching, and the sight of her graceful little body modeling his gifts in the shops of San Borja was enough to purge his mind of all the rank dust of Lurigancho.

THE DAY HE WAS SUPPOSED to leave for Frankfurt, everything appeared to be in place. He had packed summer wear beneath many layers of winter, leaving the suitcase open so that no one could doubt he was going anywhere but Germany. Dorotea had asked him to bring back a Nürnberger sausage and a bottle of 4711, and those modest requests were duly noted on a square sheet of paper that lay on his clothes like a blessing.

He had told Sophie that he would drop off the car at the body shop in Magdalena and that the mechanic would drive him the rest of the way to the airport, which wasn't far. Kissing the women and embracing his sons, he hopped into his car with a coat draped artfully over one arm and assured them he'd be back in ten days.

He was hardly down the street when he decided he would do well to stop at the supermarket and buy a few groceries for the road: The drive to Paracas would take more than three hours through a vast wilderness of dunes. He hurried into the Santa Isabel, filled a bag with fresh empanadas, and was stashing five bottles of cold pineapple soda into his cart when a woman's voice called out, "Bluhm!" He spun around to see Beatriz, Willy's wife, hurrying down the aisle toward him.

He froze, arms flared at his sides.

"What are you doing here, Bluhm? Grocery shopping, of all things! Aren't you supposed to be on a plane for Frankfurt?"

"Well, yes. I am." He looked down at the contents of his cart, trying desperately to think of some excuse.

"Don't tell me you're taking food! What are those, empanadas? You know the Germans will never let them through!"

"No, no, Beatriz. I'm taking these to my mechanic on the way to the airport. He's a hard worker and deserves a good lunch." He held his breath for a moment. "So!" he said finally. "What's Willy up to? Where's he today?"

Her forehead screwed into a frown. "With his slut, where else?"

He laughed and reached out to cuff her arm, but she recoiled. "You four protect one another, don't you, Bluhm? You're all friends with that whore, even though she's ruining his family. Even though she's drowning my children in debt. One for all, and all for one, no? Such loyal musketeers. God knows what you're doing behind Sophie's back."

So it was true. She was a little strange, just as Sophie had said. But the last thing he wanted to do now was gauge the extent of that strangeness. He gave her a quick peck on the cheek, told her he was running late, and made a fast dash for the door.

All the way to the cliffs of Miraflores, where the road cut a sharp bank south, he pondered Beatriz's words. How long had she felt betrayed by her husband's friends? And what had Bluhm ever done to merit her suspicion? Would she report him to Sophie now? Or was she so confused, so far gone, so consumed by Willy's infidelity that she saw everything through a prism of pain? He thought of these things as he drove nimbly around the grimy jitneys on Avenida Armendáriz, until he saw Maria waiting on the corner, just before the ravine, exactly where she was supposed to be. She was wearing the white summer dress with the blue and yellow flowers, and her hair was tied back with a bright yellow bow. At her feet was the striped bag he had bought for her in San Borja— packed so tight, it looked as if it might burst. She was pristine, luminous. The minute he saw her, all the unease about Beatriz—the worries about Sophie—slipped into the afternoon haze. There was only Maria. And so it would be for the next ten days.

By the time they arrived in Paracas almost four hours later, the sun had turned orange, casting a supernal glow on the houses that sat on the verdant ridge along the sea. The cottage Sophie had rented turned out to be ample and airy, with large double doors that opened directly onto the sand. It was a three-floor structure, with a large bedroom on top, a wide, roomy veranda on the second floor, and a terrace to one side, surrounded by pink fireweed and yellow lilies. An old, neglected wading pool lined with faded blue and white tiles flanked the south side of the house, and out toward the horizon, for as far as the eye could see, was the wide Pacific, rippling its way to a radiant sky.

Maria ran joyfully through the house, flinging open the doors and throwing herself on the beds, greeting each breezy room, each rattan chair, each conch-encrusted knickknack with unalloyed delight. She swung the windows wide, pointing at the unobstructed vistas as if Bluhm had never seen their equal. He followed her about, reveling in her joy, trying to see everything through her eyes, and feeling as if he, too, had been admitted to a rare world of privilege. For all the days he had spent as a bored boy on that coast, for all the magnificent summer houses his parents had rented and filled with servants, none seemed as sweet as this, in the company of this laughing girl.

They spent their days quietly, scouring the beach for shells or nestling under the striped umbrella on the terrace. Maria lined up her lucky amulets on a windowsill so that good fortune would find them and—as she put it—"wish its way through the walls." And so it did. In the mornings, when the fishermen came around with their baskets of fresh sole and shrimp, she would run out and buy just enough for a succulent lunch of ceviche and chowder. As he read the paper, she would stir milk and sugar in a pot over the stove, until it became the rich caramel of a thick, sweet dulce de leche. In the afternoons, sated by nourishment and sun, they would sit out on the veranda, where Bluhm would read her tales by Julio Ramón Ribeyro or love poems by Pablo Neruda. Come dusk, she would slip out of her clothes and curl in his lap while he drank pisco and smoked cigarettes. She would tell long stories about her brief life, about her luckless family and the many eventualities—good and bad—the fortune-teller had foreseen.

At night, he would turn on the radio, tune in to the philharmonic station, and switch off the lights, so that all they could see from their third-floor aerie was the bright eye of the radio and, through the open windows, thousands of winking stars. In that refuge, suspended between sound and sky, they would make love—often more than once in the course of one night. And in the morning before daybreak, when a pearly haze illuminated the horizon, they would run naked into the sea, until the frigid waves pushed them out again and back into the warm embrace of their bed.

He loved her hands. The way they shucked shells from shrimp, accomplishing the simplest of tasks. The way they smoothed sheets, palm down and reverentially. The way they cupped his sex, imparting her human warmth. He loved pressing each of those tiny fingers to his lips one by one before she slept, murmuring to her as if she were an infant girl, enumerating all the ways in which she pleased him.

On the fifth night, as they lay side by side, watching the

clouds move like ghostly caravels across the starlit sky, Bluhm heard the unmistakable first strains of *"Erbarme Dich"* rise toward them from the radio. He bolted upright and sat rigidly on the edge of the bed. "What's the matter?" Maria called out in alarm.

"Nothing," he said, "nothing." But the melody cut the night like a sword, making a swift course for his heart. It was the first he had thought of his family—his sons, his dead father, home. He lunged for the radio, fumbling in the dark, trying to get at the dial.

"Don't!" she yelled. "Leave it on! It's so beautiful, Carlos!"

There, squatting in shadow, he felt the tears come. He had no choice: He let them flow. They slid down his face, faster and faster as the music swelled. She sat very still, listening to the mournful cadences of that musical prayer, watching the murky outline of her lover as he crouched beside their bed, inexplicably mute. When the final note tapered off in diminuendo, then faded out at long last to absolute silence, she crept toward him. "What's wrong?"

He had no explanation. The music had come from another world, engulfing him with emotions he did not understand and for which he'd been unprepared. She lay her head on his back and wept.

SOPHIE GAVE RUDY A QUICK HUG as she ran for the telephone. He had just returned from his friend's beach house in the north and his face was a ruddy tan, his hair streaked with sun. With a backpack slung over one shoulder, he looked the very picture of well-being.

"Thank God you're back! I was worried sick—there were so many blackouts in the city."

"Fritz home?"

"Not yet!" she called back over a shoulder. "Not until to-morrow."

It was Beatriz on the telephone and, despite her agitation, Sophie managed to glean that she had something urgent to re-lay but wanted to do so in person. "I need to look at you when I tell you," Beatriz said enigmatically, and then added, "dear friend."

She seemed nervous and fidgety when she arrived, pulling at her pale, peach-colored hair, eyeing Rudy warily as she came into the living room. Rudy stood to give her a polite kiss, but she put out a hand and said, "I can't talk with you here, Rudy. I need to be alone with your mother."

"Of course," he said with a little bow. He gave Sophie a knowing wink and bolted up the stairs, taking them three at a time.

Beatriz waited until he was out of sight and then, perched on the very edge of the white sofa, with rigid fists on her knees, said what she had come to say. "I've been arguing with myself for days whether I should do this, Sophie. It's only a vague suspicion on my part, you understand. But I've seen what I've seen and, after struggling with my conscience, I've decided you should know everything. If someone had given me the courtesy of a little insight long ago, who knows? We might not be in such straits, Willy and I."

"What is it?" Sophie asked, alarmed now.

"It's about Carlos," Beatriz said, and paused to scan her friend's eyes.

"Yes?"

"Where is he?"

"In Frankfurt, Bea. You know that."

"Have you heard from him?"

"No, of course not! Telephone calls are expensive—"

"A postcard?"

"He's been away six days, Bea! You know very well it takes longer than that for mail to arrive from Europe. Now, just what are you getting at? Would you please stop asking these silly questions and tell me straight out?"

"Sophie, the day Carlos was supposed to be leaving for Germany, I saw him at the supermarket, buying empanadas and soft drinks."

"So?"

"I thought it was strange and told him so. He had some excuse. He was taking it to some car mechanic, he said."

"That makes complete sense."

"I thought so too, Sophie. Until I went out to my car, started it up, and then saw him across the lot, moving things around in the trunk of his car."

"Jesus God. You sat there and watched him?"

"Well . . . yes."

Sophie frowned.

"I did watch him, yes. And if I thought his shopping before a business trip was odd, his behavior became even stranger."

Sophie sat perfectly still.

"As I say, he was doing something in the trunk of the car. I saw him unlock his suitcase and take out his clothes. He placed about half in plastic bags. And then he took his overcoat from the front seat and tucked it into a bag as well. He arranged those bags—I think there were three or four by the time he was finished—on one side of the trunk, removed the suitcase altogether, and then threw the suitcase into the backseat." Beatriz clutched her hands and looked at her friend quizzically. "Well?" she said. "Don't you think that's bizarre?"

Sophie had to admit it was. But when she pressed Beatriz for more information, it seemed that was all the information there was. Frustrated, she threw up her hands. Beatriz stared at her long and hard and said in a steely voice, "I just pray for your sake that it's not another woman." Then she stood up abruptly and left. Sophie didn't know what to say. She couldn't thank her, couldn't be angry with her—she had been handed a riddle and would be left now to puzzle its meaning.

At first she dismissed it as more evidence of her friend's deteriorating state. A woman caught in the web of her husband's perfidy couldn't help but see others through an equivalent warp. Hadn't Bluhm told Sophie he was being driven to the airport by the mechanic? Wasn't it the most natural thing in the world to want to bring that accommodating man a reward? No, the groceries were not in the least suspicious. But putting clothes aside in plastic bags—that was something else. She had seen him pack that suitcase herself; she had seen him tuck everything in carefully.

Sitting in Bluhm's study, she realized how little she knew about this trip. She had no idea what airline he had flown, what hotel he was staying in—she couldn't come up with even one of his business contacts in Frankfurt. All she knew was the date and time of his return: Tuesday night, a little after ten. And that was a full four days away.

She looked about at her dead father-in-law's possessions: the carved desk, the embossed silver paperweights, the pre-Columbian ceramics housed carefully behind glass. Bluhm had never had his father's aptitude for money or his ease among titans of society, but he was a devoted father, a gentle man, and a good if somewhat distracted husband. She found it inconceivable that he would set out deliberately to deceive her. Beatriz had simply gone daft.

She tried putting the whole thing out of mind, yet even as she sat there she couldn't help but sift her memory for the name of Bluhm's mechanic. His shop was in Magdalena—that much she remembered—but what letter did his name start with, anyway? C? Or S? She reached for Bluhm's bookcase and pulled out the telephone directory. Thumbing her way through the automotive-service shops, she scoured all recollection for some reference point but came up with nothing— her mind a complete blank. As she stared at those listings, she saw that there were only six car-repair shops in Magdalena. She picked up Bluhm's phone and began to call them all. The first three men had never heard of Carlos Bluhm. The fourth asked her to hold while he checked the records. Yes, he said, when he came back on the line, he had done work on Mr. Bluhm's Peugeot.

"So you have it there!" she said, relieved.

There was some confusion on the other end while the man asked her to clarify what she meant. "I mean my husband's car is there in your shop right now, is it not? And you, or someone else there, drove him to the airport?"

"The airport? No, señora. This is no taxi service. My men can't spare the time to drive anyone to the airport. And, in any case, we don't have Mr. Bluhm's car."

Her fingers shaking now, she dialed the other two numbers. One didn't answer at all and, after a long while, a recorded voice told her it was no longer in service. The last shop indicated they might have Mr. Bluhm's car, but when the woman picked up the phone again, she confessed she had been mistaken: It was Mr. Blotte's car they were working on. And, furthermore—a Chevrolet.

Sophie began a frantic search of Bluhm's desk. It didn't take long for her to find the pictures, buried at the bottom of the deepest drawer. The photographs were badly lit, a murky shadow rendering a few totally undecipherable. She leafed through quickly, then went back and looked again. A dozen were of Bluhm, smiling happily—some showed him in outright laughter, his hand reaching toward the lens. The rest were of a young Indian girl Sophie didn't recognize. She seemed to be thirteen or fourteen, in a loud print dress, her long, untidy hair gathered over one shoulder. The girl's expression was not always smiling, as was Bluhm's: She was serious in one or two, staring curiously at the camera. She seemed tiny, sitting on her legs—bare toes peeking from beneath one hand.

Sophie studied the images closely, puzzling over what they could mean. As she leafed through them again, she realized that the background behind the two subjects was identical—there were windows, metal handles, tan leather seats—and then, all at once, it dawned on her that they were both sitting in Bluhm's car. She slapped the photographs down on the desk. In his car? What were he and a random child doing taking pictures in his car? Had Bluhm been trying out a new camera? Were these photographs innocent samples—nothing more?

She sat back, furious at herself for succumbing to Beatriz's paranoia. Surely there was a perfectly good explanation for his behavior in the parking lot, for her own clumsy inability to locate the mechanic, for these inexplicable photographs. She began putting Bluhm's papers back into the drawer, seeing that they were largely lading bills for the delivery of equipment or letters requesting service and spare parts, when suddenly a folded sheet slipped out from among them. She was about to tuck the document back into the pile but opted instead to unfold it, so that it would lay uniformly flat, with all the others. It did not appear to be a bill or letter. It was a simple handwritten list, headed by two letters, *S* and *M*. Part of it was crossed out and annotated, but a quick scan of the items surrendered no immediate meaning—until, under the letter *S*, she saw the word *Tuberoses*. And then a little farther up in the same column: *Good mother to her sons*. In one illuminating moment she understood that *S* signified *Sophie*—it could not be otherwise. And then came the rush of everything else: the virtues of a woman named *M*, the raw sexuality of the appraisals, the cruelty of the cold-blooded comparisons, the incontestable verdict of *Dry* and *Wet*.

Sophie stood, and the whole accumulation of paper fell from her lap, slapping the floor with resounding finality. She ran from the room, looking for Dorotea, who was reading peacefully on the long white couch in the living room. "My God, Sophie. What on earth?"

"It's Carlos," she said, unable to restrain herself. "And another woman."

Her mother-in-law blanched.

Dorotea was disbelieving at first, but when Sophie took her into the study and showed her the writing in Bluhm's own hand, she could only shake her head in wonder. It was so puerile and vicious: the *NULL in bed* versus *Curious i. b.*; the stark counterpoint of *Day* and *Night*. Suddenly Dorotea had the sickening feeling she didn't know her own son. She could understand the male urge to stray from marriage. God knew her father had been bitten by the impulse. He had even sent her, as an eight-year-old girl, to knock on doors with letters for his mistresses. Perhaps even her husband, Rodolfo, had succumbed to those lures. She had always feared it. But what lunacy had possessed Carlos to write it all down? And so sadistically!

She took Sophie's hands in hers. "Schätze, I'm so sorry. I can't imagine what's gotten into him, but you must understand, these things happen. Men try to prove their manhood. It doesn't mean a thing. It's not about love. He loves you! He loves his sons! If it's true about this woman, believe me, it's just a fleeting thing." She stopped there, letting the message sink in. But the expressions of sympathy only made Sophie more miserable. She burst into bitter tears. Would she ever survive the insult? The indignity and the shame?

Dorotea felt her anger rise as her daughter-in-law wept freely, but she tried to remain calm and rational. She hunted through the pictures, searching for concrete clues. "So who's this?" she asked Sophie, tapping the girl's face with a relentless finger.

"I don't know, Mutti!" Sophie cried. "For all I know, she's his bastard child!"

"Now, now," said Dorotea, and patted the ragged woman on her arms. "Let's not jump to ridiculous conclusions." She was silent for a while, then tried to work out her son's whereabouts, reasoning it all aloud. "Well, he's either with this M woman in Germany or, perhaps, not in Germany at all. He's probably right here in town, holed up God knows where."

Sophie looked up, wiping the tears from her face. "Mutti," she said slowly. "I know where he is."

"Where?"

"In the beach house I rented for us. In Paracas."

THE LAST FOUR DAYS were quiet, uneventful, marking the profound comfort the two lovers felt together. Curious, yet wary about asking too much, they reached that perfect equilibrium of sympathies that only new love can bring. So tranquil were their days that they began to count them by the smallest of wonders. One day it was an egret, making its lone, fitful progress along the breaking waves. The next it was a condor, wheeling north by northeast, inland toward the cordillera. And so on—an agile dolphin, a scuttling crab—until they reached the day when they would witness these things no more: when they needed to shutter the house and head back to the city.

Bluhm needed to get back in time to buy his mother a bottle of 4711. He knew he could find one at a grossly inflated price at the perfume shop on Conquistadores. The Nürnberger sausage was another matter: He'd had to call a friend, an importer of Alpine products he knew from countless functions at the Club Germania. As it happened, his friend had several varieties of sausage on hand and urged Bluhm to stop by and choose one.

He and Maria held hands for much of the drive—for three hours of afternoon sun until nightfall, when the reflected halo of light over Lima rushed toward them through the dark. For all the happy babble they had exchanged at the beach, for all the noisy love, they were mute now, as if nothing more could be said, nothing further negotiated. Listening to the radio, they learned that a bomb had exploded on one of the capital's streets, unsuccessfully targeting the country's attorney general. Little by little they reentered their difficult world—a place that could make no promises. Shortly after eight, he dropped her off on Angamos, a convenient thoroughfare for buses to Lurigancho. As they parted, Bluhm worked out a system: If the telephone in his house rang only once, he would assume it was she, trying to reach him. He would then call the public telephone by her front door as soon as he possibly could. They kissed tenderly, pressing each other to their hearts, unwilling to end their rapture. When she finally boarded the bus for Lurigancho and glanced back at him over her shoulder, he saw that her eyes were shining with love.

At ten, after a glass of beer with the friend who had furnished the sausage, he headed home with his winter clothes neatly stashed in his suitcase, the bratwurst and cologne on top, and his overcoat on the passenger seat by his side. Nearing the Golf Club, he felt a slight flutter in his stomach, a rising nervousness about how to recount a trip that had never been. Surely his mother would want a full report on every restaurant he had frequented, every veal chop and spaetzle consumed. Sophie would wonder why he hadn't brought her a souvenir, and then, in time, would appreciate his frugality. He spent these last minutes reviewing everything he remembered about Frankfurt—the old brick of the rebuilt opera house, the cozy Ebbelwei taverns with their gargantuan steins of ale, the museums nestling along the Main, the Kaiserdom, the Paulskirche...

He pulled into the driveway and unlocked the gate—the scent of the night-blooming Mirabilis filled his senses, welcoming him home. It wasn't until he had shut off the engine and hauled his suitcase over the slate walk that he noted how dark the house was. The front windows were black on both floors. Had there been a bomb in San Isidro, a power failure? But no, the gardens up and down the street were illuminated, the houses brightly lit. Perhaps the boys were at the beach with their friends, Sophie reading in the back, Dorotea asleep under her eiderdown.

He turned his key in the lock and stepped into the darkness. Running his hands along the wall, he found the light switch and flipped it. The immediate glare was blinding, but as his eyes adjusted he saw that the massive, marble-topped table in the entryway was gone, as were the leather chairs—as was every stick of furniture, every family painting. The room was bare. Four feet ahead, on the tile floor, was an envelope. He picked it up. It was addressed in tidy letters: *CARLOS BLUHM*.

He raced through the empty corridor into the living room, switching on lights as he went. Everywhere he saw only blank walls and a vast, cavernous space. There were nails where paintings had hung. Geometric discolorations where rugs had once lay. The dining room had no table. The kitchen, no pots. The study had been liberated of all contents except for the telephone, a pile of cameras on the floor, an untidy stack of paper. Upstairs, he had been left a bed, a few sheets and towels, his toiletries, clothes. Everything else was gone—the rooms yawning, one after another, as he stumbled through them in stupefaction and horror.

Mouth dry, heart pounding, he sat on the bed and tore open the letter. Inside was a single sheet of paper. The script was small and orderly, written in his wife's hand.

Carlos,

    By now you have seen that we are gone. And by now, perhaps, you are feeling something like the emptiness you bore into my heart when I realized where you have been these last ten days and with whom.

A call to the rental agency confirmed it. They told me you had come to the office in person, paid cash, and picked up the keys. They couldn't tell me, of course, in whose company you were spending your beach vacation. It took your son to do that.

Fritz looked at the photographs of you and the girl and told us he recognized her from the supermarket. (The supermarket!) It seems you had given him the courtesy of an introduction to Señorita Juana Maria Fernandez. When I checked with the management at Santa Isabel, they informed me she had been fired for delinquent attendance. If she was off with you in that pretty little house in Paracas, I can certainly understand why.

Santa Isabel's records show the girl's age as 22, but Willy tells me they are wrong. She is 16—younger than your youngest son—and that fact is nowhere more evident than in those pictures you took of her in our car. We haven't told any of this to the boys, of course, but your mother and I are outraged (as you can imagine) by what we've learned: the lies, the willful duplicity, the perversion. There's no need for me to mention the appalling list comparing me to your child lover, but I do it here so that you can know the extent of the affront.

I have moved Dorotea and the boys with me to the house my parents have just finished building across from them in La Molina. They had intended to rent it, but these are hard times and, in any case, they are all too willing to forgo the income for now. As you see, I have taken the furniture, which is rightly your mother's, and left you the house. I

*told Dorotea that there was no way I could stay there a day
longer. She opted to come with me. You know how she loves
her grandsons.*

*I think it's best if you leave us alone for a while. In any
case, the boys will spend the rest of the summer with cousins
and friends. I've taken all the bills and expect I'll have to sell
some things in order to pay them off. So even where
financial matters are concerned, there is no need for us to
communicate. I leave the maintenance of that house entirely
in your hands. (I should add that Manuela, too, has decided
to come away with us.)*

*So there you have it, Carlos. I will not argue with you
about this. I will not seek my revenge through lawyers. And
I will not stoop to call you names. I simply cannot continue
to live under the same roof with someone who has crossed so
many lines of rectitude and decency.*

S.

Bluhm sat on the denuded bed, motionless. There was a
gentle tap at the far window—a large moth throwing its soft
body against the bright glass. For minutes or hours he remained inert, imagining his wife pawing through his desk and
coming upon the list. He pictured the scenes that must have
followed: his mother's face in grim, resolute disapproval; his
son connecting the photographs with a girl seen long ago at a
cash register. Was it possible? Had his orderly life been un-
done, all of these rooms emptied, because of a few bits of
paper—because he had scribbled something out of caprice?
Was there no recourse, no argument, no possible defense?

The first thing he did when bafflement gave way to fury was to run downstairs and call Willy, despite the late hour. The insurance agent answered the phone with a small, wary hello. "Bluhm!" he erupted when he heard his friend's voice. "Oh, God, Bluhm. I'm so sorry, old friend."

"Sorry?" Bluhm screamed. "For turning your back on me? For being a disgusting little fuck of a traitor?"

There was a long silence before Willy spoke again. "She knew everything, Carlos. I didn't say anything she didn't already know. For Chrissake, she knew the girl's name, where she worked, what she looked like! She knew things I didn't know: I thought you were in Germany, eating strudel! She knew you were out in Pisco or Paracas, or wherever the hell you two went to sun your asses."

"But did you have to tell her Maria's age?" Bluhm was clutching his head, unable to comprehend what was happening to him. A sob left his chest and filled his throat.

"Bluhm," Willy responded immediately now. "I'm coming over. You wait there, I'll—"

"No! I don't want to see you, Brenner! Don't get ideas! I never want to see your asshole face again!" He slammed down the phone and sat on the floor, his whole body trembling.

Eventually he went back upstairs, took a hot shower, lay on the unmade bed, tried to sleep. But as night wore on, all he could do was lie there, stare at the ceiling, think of his sons, and wonder how in the world to fix it all. How to reverse this terrible tide, recover the life that had slipped so swiftly and irrevocably through his fingers?

In the morning, he threw open the windows so that he

could smell the garden. It was the only space she hadn't ravaged, his only refuge from the vacant walls, the endless desert of floors. Calmed by that perfume, he decided to go to his in-laws' in La Molina, call on his wife, try to apologize. Surely she would forgive him. When nine o'clock finally came, he dialed his mother-in-law's number.

"Carlos," Señora Westermann said stiffly. "I thought it might be you."

"Señora, I want to see Sophie right away, this morning."

"She won't see you, Carlos. She is very serious about this. Frankly, her father and I don't blame her one bit. We find your behavior...that child...the whole thing...repellent. Shocking. But that's beside the point. She has given us strict orders."

"I'll come see my mother, then!"

"Dorotea won't see you either. She told me this herself last night. It's very grave with her, Carlos, very grave."

"Grave? What in God's name do you mean?"

"I mean she's very angry at you. And disgusted. And worried about Sophie. I worry about Sophie too, Carlos. Her father and I don't want you to do anything to upset her any more than you already have. She's very delicate right now. She hasn't eaten for days!"

Bluhm received this last bit of information in silence, not because of its inherent importance but because it was here that he began to truly understand the significance of the moment, the abrupt terminus of his marriage. He had been the architect of its dismantling. He had broken his own rule—plunged so deep into a relationship that he'd leveled his known world. Everything would change from here forward. Everything. This house would never be the same: His wife and mother were gone, sharing a closer bond than he'd ever been able to forge with either one of them. His sons would grow into men under other people's roofs, and, looking back, they would blame him for their expulsion from that Eden. He would be the betrayer for the rest of their lives.

Never had he felt so alienated, so forsaken. He looked around for something familiar, something to anchor him, but there was nothing. Only the faraway bark of a dog.

He had little to lose. When Maria signaled with a lone ring later that morning, he did not hesitate. He called back instantly. He listened to her tell him that Lima Nights was closed—Jose Ferrari had been killed by a car bomb as he pulled up in front of a bank to deposit the week's earnings. A random murder. A man in the wrong place at the wrong time. She no longer had a job.

"Pack your things," he heard himself say. "Take a taxi, come to the house. You can stay as long as you need to. Everyone's gone." He gave her the address. She didn't ask what had happened; she didn't indicate that she already knew perfectly well where the house was. She took down all the information and promised she would be there before five.

She was there well before one. He was sitting on the second-floor veranda, where he had spent much of the morning listening to the doves, hearing Rudy's music in his head, imagining Fritz diving through waves at the Roedenbeck beach house, when he saw a dilapidated yellow Volkswagen beetle come to a rumbling halt in front of the house. She emerged from the taxi's backseat, carrying the colorful tote he had given her, a bulging plastic bag, and a worn pink box from which she took a number of bills to pay the driver.

Bluhm rushed to the hallway and pressed the buzzer that released the lock in the iron gate. Speaking into the intercom, he instructed her to push the right gate open and then pull it tight behind her.

By the time he got to the front door, she was halfway up the walk, staring up at the house as she dragged the large bag over the flat stones. She was squinting at the windows, twisting her head this way and that, trying to see through the glare in the panes. She seemed resolute, intent on registering every detail. He was pleased by what he took as awe, although he noted there was something else too: She was largely mute, surprisingly subdued. Once he had helped her bring her things into the entryway and set them on the floor, she moved cautiously through that enormous hall, down the corridor, and into the empty living room. He followed her.

"Well?" he said finally, when he could stand her silence no longer.

"It looks so different," she whispered.

"Different? Different from what?" he asked, confused.

"From before."

"How would you know what it looked like before? You've never been here!"

That was when she began running from room to room, opening doors, needing to verify the monumental emptiness. "Where is the marble table with all the flowers!" she cried. "The rugs! The paintings! The big, shiny white sofa! The piano with its wing in the air?" She seemed genuinely panicked, as if she had lost these things herself. Bluhm wondered what diabolical power had given her the ability to picture furniture she'd never seen.

And then, all at once, he realized the obvious: She had seen it before. She had come there to see how he lived. She had stood in the street with her face pressed against the iron and taken count of his possessions. She had wanted this house so much that she had pictured herself in it, imagined herself behind its windows, wished her way through its walls.

Part Two

MANO A MANO

AUTUMN 2006

• • •

They are equally matched, superbly equipped
by life in the arena.
See them perform mano a mano, against the great
horned beast of their fate.

—Poster, Plaza de Toros
Lima, Peru

6

Spears

TERCIO DE VARAS

CARMELA WAS JUST GOING DOWNSTAIRS AS BLUHM started to go up, and, in one of those unavoidably awkward moments, he stopped midway, edged toward the wall, and let the large woman pass. "I know! I know!" she yelled over one shoulder. It was galling enough that she carried on in his house as if it were her own, but that she should shriek like a fishwife was more than he could bear. He put his hands over his ears.

"When I come back, I'll have some answers for you, I swear!" she added. She was breathing hard, face lit with perspiration, her high-heeled shoes betraying her heft with ear-splitting reports.

"You have a problem with me, Bluhm? Yes or no?" She was at the foot of the staircase now, glaring back at him, two fists on her barrel hips. He shook his head and waved a hand, willing her to disappear. "Old crab!" Carmela muttered. "Some

nerve you have covering your ears. After all I do for her!" He
turned his back, trudged on. At the second-floor landing, he
heard the front door slam, sending a shiver through the decay-
ing mansion.

He pulled his cardigan around him and fastened its buttons. The first winter fog had rolled in from the sea and a
piercing cold had invaded the house, leaving a slick layer of
moisture underfoot, on the walls, on the banister—on every
possible surface. He stepped onto the landing cautiously, re-
calling last year's misfortune: He had slipped and fallen in the
dark, hammering his chin as he descended, fracturing a rib.
He'd had to stay in bed for a week.

If asked, he could have given a rich account of each swollen
joint, each winter grippe that had had its way with his waning
body. But he would have been unable to give a similar reckoning of his heart. It was as if he were living two different lives:
one in real time, another in limbo. He was keenly aware of the
stiffness in his knees, the shrinking girth of his chest, the soft
little pot of his belly, but he couldn't quite say why he had lived
with the woman upstairs for twenty years, or even how he felt
about her, really. The days had slipped by. That was all.

He didn't dwell on it much. With all the demands of his
daily job, the pending bills, the constant household disasters,
there were always more-pressing cares. But from time to time,
Willy or Oscar or Marco would say, "You've got to be kidding
me, Bluhm, she's still there?" And he would shrug his shoulders. "What can I do? She's like an old pillow. Too worn to use.
Too comfortable to throw away." And they would laugh; and
years would pass.

The house, too, had felt the rudeness of time, and its flaws and infirmities cried out in its squealing doors, its creaking wood, its sighing walls, when the winds blew down from the cordillera. The iron gate was pocked by rust; the handsome veranda, stooped by gravity. It was no longer the elegant manse of his spirited middle age. No longer the living museum of his father's and grandfather's achievements. Left to fall into disrepair, eroded by too many seasons of dust and fog, the place was a hull now—a tottering ruin of old republican glory.

Maria was in her room, peering into the mirror, rimming her eyes with kohl. The afternoon's telenovela was blaring from her dresser. *"No! No! That can't be true!"* a desperate voice was saying. *"I was with him an hour ago and he was so loving to me! So full of tenderness and affection!"* Seeing Bluhm's reflection loom suddenly in the mirror, Maria gave a start and spun around in her chair. She was wearing her pink flannel housecoat and light blue slippers. Three large rollers marched back from her forehead, holding her short copper hair. She had grown somewhat thicker with the passing years, but she was a handsome woman with a strikingly chiseled face.

"You want something?" she said.

"It's what I don't want that bothers me. I don't want that insufferable woman in my house! Why is it that even though Willy has managed to get rid of her, I have to go on seeing her face under my roof?"

"I live here too."

The dialogue in the telenovela had reached a fevered pitch and the music was spiraling to match. Bluhm was forced to shout, pointing a finger at the television. "There's something else I don't want! Can't you turn it down, for God's sake? My family lived in this house for more than a hundred years and we never had to put up with one of those moronic boxes. Shut it off!"

"This is where I live now. I'll do as I please." She walked up and closed the door.

Bluhm sighed and went to his room. It was Saturday, his day off from the appliance store. Having to live all week with the cacophony of competing television sets, sound systems, and the whir of kitchen devices, he had come to treasure silence—to look forward to the quiet green of his San Isidro garden, where he could listen to the doves coo. He closed the door, went to the double window, and threw open the glass. It was a typical winter day: There was a deathlike stillness, a fine mist, and—past the stately cherimoya—a gray and marbled sky. A chauffeured car coasted down the street, sleek and soundless as a shark. Across the way, over the walls, he could see into the well-tended compound of an American diplomat. A gardener began pruning the bougainvillea and a fitful clack invaded the afternoon calm.

Not one neighbor remained who could remember his marriage to Sophie. They had all moved on, either to more modest, more secure houses in Miraflores or out of the country altogether, to better opportunities elsewhere. It was just as well. Bluhm's exchanges with them had always been chilly—they were haughty people, accustomed to far grander lifestyles than he had ever been able to afford. But when Sophie evacuated the place, all communication had stopped.

A man abandoned by wife and mother? In this Catholic country? How could that possibly be? And then there was the question of the brown girl: At first, they took her for a servant. It was she, after all, whom they saw sweeping the walkway, chatting with guards and domestics, singing as she hosed down the veranda. But as time wore on, they could see that Bluhm's house was filling up with shoddy, inelegant furniture; that the *chola* had people even more humble to do her bidding; that she could be seen at the front door in her nightgown, throwing kisses as Bluhm came and went. That was the point at which any pretense of civility ceased. They started to worry about the effects of Bluhm's profligacy on their own real estate. They stood out on the street—men by their cars, elderly couples with their arms crossed—scowling through the ironwork as if their accumulated umbrage could bring back a vanished past. And then, with the years, they moved on, surrendering their houses to foreigners who didn't know the difference.

There was a time, early on, when Bluhm would have sold the house gladly, rented a smaller place so that he could put cash in the bank. But that was at the height of the terrorist grip on the city, when selling would have been impossible. Eventually the government found and arrested the Shining Path's leader, dispersed the terrorists, and sent them whimpering to the jungle. Bluhm mentioned to Marco that it might be good now to get rid of the house, buy something a little less grand. He had no job, after all—hadn't had one for almost a year, since the German manufacturers had pulled out of that nervous market. But Marco, who knew something about real

estate, told Bluhm he was not to sell the house under any circumstances, no matter what chance misfortune befell him. It
was the only financial security he had. That was when Bluhm
decided to take a job as manager of camera sales in the clam-
orous Hiraoka emporium.

It was remarkable, really, how well his three friends had
fared over the years. Marco had gone from the financial ruin
of the Cesar Hotel to the top job at the towering Marriott, and
had married a young socialite to boot. Willy had finally left
Carmela, returned wholeheartedly to Beatriz, and become a
doting, jolly grandfather. Oscar, after the publication of his
celebrated book, *Sirens of the Mind,* had given up his psychi-
atric practice to become dean of the medical school at the
University of San Marcos. Even the Club Germania—broker
of Teutonic bonds, custodian of ethnic memory—was a different, more elevated institution now: a place for families preoccupied with language education. Not a watering hole for
restless men.

SHE TOOK OUT THE ROLLERS, tucked them into a drawer,
and brushed her hair neatly around the ears, spiking the
crown with gel. Every hair was in place, the total effect pleasing. But she could also see something pinched about her eyes,
a hard line to her lips—an emerging mask of worry. Carmela's
visit had been more than a little disturbing. Was it true that
Bluhm was seeing another woman? That he had been seeing
other women for years? And that was the reason he refused to

talk about her role in his life, refused to seek out a priest, refused to make her a full partner in marriage?

Maria had been worried about it for some months now. Every time he left the house freshly groomed, his collar splashed with cologne, she'd wondered what new salesgirl he was trying to impress. She had had passing temptations herself—the handsome chauffeur next door, the too-friendly electrician. But she had never been unfaithful to Bluhm; she had known what there was to lose.

She switched off the television, slipped on a sweater, tied a bright scarf around her neck. "Don't you know," Carmela had said, "that before you came along, he had a different girl every week! I spent a good chunk of my life with those four— I ought to know! What on God's earth made you think he could change?"

"He's older now," Maria had said, "calmer." And then she added, "So am I."

"Pah!" Carmela scoffed. "Men don't change. They may alter a quirk here and there to fool you, take up a hobby, but they don't deviate from their basic natures. Just look at Willy! Always a family man. When he wanted to play around, what did he do? He put me in an apartment! He couldn't bring himself to sleep with every tramp he met, the way the others did. I watched them all hop around like fleas! No. He made me into his vision of what sex should be: dependable, homey, and under his own roof. What I didn't understand at the time was how soon it would all end: Whenever the rent stopped, the roof would be gone. Poof! Finished! And that's exactly what happened. He stopped paying rent, kicked over my whole world, and went back to his family. Just as Bluhm has gone back to his old ways."

"You know this for a fact, Carmela? You've seen it?"

"Believe me, honey, I know what I'm talking about." She sat back and clucked her tongue. "You sleep in separate rooms, yes or no?"

"You know the answer."

"Well, let me say something about that. A bed on the other side of his wall won't get you what you want. I've been meaning to tell you that for a while."

Maria tried to argue, but Carmela barreled ahead. "You're still young! You still have your looks! Why have you given up? Why are you throwing it all away? Just look at you in that robe. And those raggedy slippers! Bluhm didn't fall for a woman who looked like that! You were always so turned out, Maria, so sharp. You can't afford not to be! You need to work at it! There are plenty of *cholas* who'd like to live in this big house, have what you have!" She fixed Maria with her eyes, let the lesson sink in.

The words had stung. As Maria leaned into the mirror, she couldn't avoid the simple calculation: If Bluhm could throw over a wife of twenty-one years, he could throw over a mistress of twenty. The thought pricked her brain and rode her veins freely, like a disease.

In the beginning, Maria suspected it was only a matter of time before Bluhm would go back to his wife. But two years later, when his mother died and the wife made no effort to comfort him, Maria understood that the marriage was truly over, that any sympathies between them were unrecoverable.

Sophie had died too, three years after that—of a swift and terrible cancer. Maria managed to contain her joy and wait for Bluhm to raise the question of marriage, but when several months passed and he did not, she decided to propose it herself: "Why don't we get married, Carlos? You're a widower now, aren't you? Even the church would approve!" Bluhm didn't say no; he didn't say yes. The question just hung between them, like fog.

A few weeks later he surprised her with a tiny amethyst ring and announced their engagement. She was ecstatic, bustling about the house in happy anticipation. But the years wore on and he never took it any further. His oldest son had found a wife. The youngest too. Three grandsons entered the world. And the stone just sat on her finger. That was when she decided she could be equally stubborn, equally withholding. She moved to a different room.

"You need to work at it!" Carmela had said, but all Maria had done since she stepped foot in that house was to work against countless obstacles. Even after two decades, the memory of her first day at 300 Avenida Rivera was vivid: the scolding emptiness, the gaping void. She had sat on the floor, on the steps, in the garden—waiting endless hours for a plastic table, a rattan sofa, two hard aluminum chairs. They had sold the old Peugeot, which made it possible to furnish the first floor, but Bluhm had been inconsolable, mourning that car as if it were a lost limb.

And then there were the neighbors. The only person in San Isidro who seemed happy to see her was the soldier Pérez, who came bounding across the street to welcome her.

But even he had trouble concealing his shock when she told him that she had not only moved into the house, she'd moved into the master's bedroom. The others made their outrage plain, especially the crone with the stiff puce hair, who strolled by and hissed through the gate as if Maria were a zoo animal. Maria would retaliate by singing at the top of her lungs, or emptying scrub water over the fence, or standing on the front stoop in a flimsy nightgown, throwing kisses at Bluhm. It felt good to rattle them. When Bluhm wasn't there, she'd goad them on purpose: roaming the garden in her night-clothes, scratching herself. She loved to see their startled faces. She'd been such a child.

But the hardest obstacle turned out to be her body. Try as she might to become pregnant by Bluhm—to create a living, breathing human bridge between them—she hadn't been able to. She had spent a week eating nothing but artichokes, as the midwives in Lurigancho had advised her to do. She had wrapped herself in warm, freshly ironed towels, lured Bluhm to bed, and stayed on her back, cradling their union. She had gone to the fortune-teller and asked for special amulets, candles, prayer cards—anything that might bring her luck in this—but the man only shook his head and said that some hybrids were not meant to be. It was like trying to cross a chicken with a goose. They had no traits, no breed in common. "All I can see," the fortune-teller said squarely to Maria, "is blank eggs in the straw."

"Señora."

Maria looked up. It was her maid, knocking timidly at the door. "What is it, Flavia?"

"Señora, your husband has asked me to make him another pot of hot coffee. Shall I give you a cup as well?"

Maria opened the door. The girl was on the fair side, with naturally ruddy cheeks. She had high hips, small breasts, and a meek way of looking down at the floor when spoken to. Standing there, clutching the tray with rough hands, her bright blue uniform voluminous around her, she seemed straightforward and guileless, not at all the sort of female who could provoke the slightest interest in a man. But Carmela's warning had found its mark.

"Hand me that tray, Flavia, and go back to the kitchen. I'll take this in to Mr. Bluhm."

TOO MUCH TIME HAD PASSED, too many marriages broken, for the four friends to gather with their wives, as they once had. Oscar's wife had put it in no uncertain terms: The dirty *chola* was not to step foot in her house. The breezy holiday parties had stopped altogether. Marco's new wife confessed that she thought Bluhm the most charming of all his friends and, despite Marco's protestations, had considered inviting Bluhm's woman to a fund-raiser for the poor and homeless of Lima. But the more she thought about it, the less she could recall seeing dark-skinned people at any of those affairs, except, of course, as staff. And as for Beatriz, she was far too devoted to Sophie—and then Sophie's memory—to even contemplate being in the same room with that tart.

So for five years the men had been convening once a month

in the second-floor bar of the Marriott. Marco would play the expansive host and reserve the best corner, alert the waitresses, order all drinks on the house. The four had been tamed by the years; they were no longer habitués of Lima's dance joints or bordellos, happy merely to watch pretty girls bring them their well-chilled martinis. There, in comfortable, upholstered chairs, gazing out at the rolling Pacific, they would sit for an hour or two and try valiantly to fortify their ties.

It was at one of those gatherings on a gray, wintry night, as Bluhm was warming his veins with gin, that the conversation turned to his son Rudy.

"What a pleasure it was to see him," Marco commented brightly. "He's turned into a fine man, Bluhm! With a beautiful family!"

"Rudy was at the hotel today?" Bluhm said incredulously.

"Right over there," Marco replied. "With a party of thirty or so, for your grandson's tenth birthday."

"God! I had no idea he had that kind of money," Bluhm sighed. "Lunch for so many people," he spread his hands, "here!"

"But he's running his father-in-law's business now," said Willy. "He's the head of the company. Surely you knew that, Bluhm."

"No! Really? I knew he was working there, but I had no idea he was in charge. Who would guess that a glass company could be such a moneymaker?"

"You've got to be kidding!" Oscar exclaimed. "Just look at this building. All glass. The construction industry is booming. That young man of yours is sitting on a fortune!"

Bluhm shook his head. In such ways did he get word of his boys. His friends knew more about them than he did. At first, when Fritz and Rudy were younger, Sophie had sent invitations to their graduations, weddings, their first grandchild's baptism, but the cards were addressed pointedly to him only, with the clear understanding that he was to come alone. He had attended the first two or three events, if only to peck his own mother on the cheek when she offered it to him woodenly. But he could see how uncomfortable it made his sons to have him in the same room with Sophie. They were so obviously pained, so overly polite that it stung his heart. As for Sophie, she would be rigid from the moment he walked in to the moment he walked out, looking more wan and pitiful by the year. He decided then, for everybody's sake, not to attend those functions at all and simply send congratulatory notes or gifts. But two years went by and suddenly his mother was gone. Fritz had called to tell him so—Dorotea had died peacefully in her bed, just before her eightieth birthday. Bluhm made an exception and went to her funeral. And then three years after that, Fritz made another call and relayed three stunning facts in a row: Sophie was dead after a fierce bout with breast cancer; Rudy's first child was due any day; Fritz had been promoted to partner in his law firm. The news startled Bluhm into silence. He'd been prepared for his mother's passing, but he hadn't imagined Sophie would die.

Even after the two aggrieved women had left this earth and climbed to the eternal hereafter, communication with his sons had not improved. Fritz and Rudy were busy, prosperous men now, with growing families to distract them—and, in any case, they had grown accustomed to life without Bluhm. The odd thing was: He had no regrets. Oh, there were times he wished he could sit with his boys as he used to do, muss their hair, make pilsner, listen to the cello, but he could summon no tenderness for his truncated marriage, no vestigial affection for their mother. He couldn't recall what had attracted him to her in the first place. Her Teutonic pedigree? His father's approval? And then a whole lifetime had gone by—a spooling blur of too many years—and the only thing he had to show for it was Maria.

"Say, Bluhm!" Willy said, after they'd gone around the circle talking about their wives. "How's that little girl of yours?"

"Still badgering you about marriage, I bet," Marco added, giving his shoulder a companionable nudge.

"Some things never change," Bluhm answered with a smile. "She works her side of the battlefield. I work mine." They laughed at that, but he could sense their discomfort.

"How many years have you been together, Bluhm?" Oscar asked, after some silence.

"Twenty. Nearly as long as Sophie and I lived under one roof." He stopped there and looked around at his friends—all happily married now, all far more prosperous than he. He felt suddenly small, inadequate. He took a toothpick and plunged it into his drink, lancing a fat green olive.

"It's the house, I bet," Marco said. "That's why you haven't married her. You don't want to risk it," he added approvingly. "And besides, she's a bloody Indian. It makes perfect sense to me."

"She deserves some security," Bluhm said sadly. "She had

quite a life before she met me. She's an Indian, yes, but she's come far, you know."

"What about that brother of hers?" Oscar asked.

"Which one? She has two." The men shot one another guilty looks. They hadn't really listened to Bluhm's accounts of her melodramas; they weren't conversant in the details. They had forgotten that Freddy had disappeared at the height of the terror, that Pablito now worked on and off as a dock loader in Callao, that her father had been killed by her mother's lover, that her mother had died of tuberculosis a few months after Maria moved in.

They were momentarily quiet, all too aware of the deep chasm that divided them from Bluhm now. He had stepped over that chasm briefly, only to maroon himself on the other side. He scanned their faces, reading their minds. "You ask why I don't marry again, Oscar? Some form of cowardice, probably. I'm amazed she's stuck with me as long as she has. I drive her crazy. She drives me crazy. It can't be easy living with an old coot like me. She could be out in the world, bearing a young man's children, raising a family—"

"Oh, for Chrissake!" Marco exploded. "Are you getting soft in the head? That woman came out of the mud! They live like pigs up there in those hills! Have you forgotten that, Bluhm? You gave her the good life. She's never had to lift a finger!"

"Shut up, Marco!" Willy said. He turned to his old friend and spoke warmly. "I understand, Bluhm. I really do. That house has been in your family for generations! You're right to hold on to it for your boys. And who knows? If Sophie had forgiven you, things might have turned out differently. You didn't start out thinking Maria was forever. You just wanted a little ass." He leaned in, put his elbows on his knees. "We have a name for you in the insurance business, Bluhm: You're a baseline customer, a person who sticks with the minimum and won't invest more. That's where you are with Maria. You're sticking with the minimum because you never saw her as a wife. You never will." Bluhm opened his mouth to speak, but Willy went on. "The truth is, I really admire you. I admire your absolute lack of prejudice. There aren't many men who would give up what you once had, least of all for a woman of her race. Marco thinks you won't marry her because of her skin. Well, he's wrong. You've already crossed that line. You won't marry her because you never meant to. That's all."

The words brought Oscar to his feet. "Herr Doktor!" he crowed, raising an empty glass to Willy. The psychiatrist was beaming, his tall figure illuminated by the flickering lights in the window. "Come around to the university, old boy! We need to give you a goddamn chair!"

THEIR CONVERSATION LINGERED in Oscar's mind well after the four embraced and parted. The doctor thought about Maria as he drove back to his sleek glass house on the cliff of Barranco. In all the years she had lived with Bluhm, only Oscar, among Bluhm's friends, had had any contact with her, and each occasion was fresh in memory, alive in his mind's eye.

The first had occurred by chance late one night, fourteen

years before. Oscar had been with a group of psychiatrists at the Club Nacional in downtown Lima. After a genial meal, his colleagues had repaired to their cars and roared off toward the suburbs. But the old city center was no longer what it had been—the area was rank with thieves. As Oscar ambled to his car, slightly under the influence, he'd been roughed up by three burly thugs, his face bloodied, his wallet and cell phone stolen. In his panic, he'd lost his way home and, finding himself in San Isidro, stopped at Bluhm's to collect his wits.

When Maria opened the gate, the vision of that fully mature woman surprised him. She was in tight jeans and a sweater, her hair in a ponytail, her face strikingly handsome. She immediately assessed what had happened and led him straightaway to Bluhm. As the three settled into Bluhm's study, she daubed his wound and washed away the blood. She told him she had done as much for her brothers many times and spoke of her old neighborhood with a wisdom he hadn't imagined she'd have, a keen intelligence. She squeezed his arm and asked if he wanted some strong coffee, and when she delivered it, bending over to set his cup on the table, he couldn't help note the fullness of her breasts, the perfect little V of her pubis. Lifting away the tray, she accidentally grazed him with one hip and he was struck by her animality—the way her heat filled the room. But she hovered over Bluhm too, stroked his hands, asked if there was anything he needed. And Oscar found himself imagining—well beyond a psychiatrist's professional curiosity—what sex was like between them.

Oscar saw her once more on a summer's day, many years later. He had dashed through an expensive department store, in search of a gift for his wife's birthday, when he spotted a pretty woman trying on scarves before a full-length mirror. She was dark, small, and well built, with an ass like an inverted heart. As she slid the luxurious silk over her bare arms and glanced over one shoulder, he saw it was Bluhm's woman. He might have said hello, but something in her expression stopped him. She seemed lost in another world, suspended in fantasy. He watched as she turned this way and that, imagining herself someone she was not. He couldn't help but wonder: Who was she, really? And what was it like for her in that big house? Who were her friends?

By the time his wife's present was wrapped and paid for, he had made up his mind. He would say hello—invite her for a quick cortado at Manolo's, get to know her better. But when he looked up from the cash register, she was gone.

MARIA KNEW VERY WELL that Bluhm had a low tolerance for Carmela, so, with a mix of defiance and desperation, she had cultivated her over the years. She had no other friends. Her only opportunity for casual conversation was with servants along the Avenida Rivera, but nothing had ever come of that fleeting solidarity. Carmela, who now worked as a caretaker for two dowager sisters in Miraflores, had become her closest confidante, and Carmela's regular Saturday visits her lifeline to the world.

"So, tell me again," Carmela said the following week. "You went looking to give him a good time and he ignored you?"

"I took some coffee into his bedroom," Maria sighed. "I don't want that girl fawning over him anymore. I know her kind. I know what she's after."

"And?"

"Well, I got on his bed, took off my shoes, and made him a little invitation."

"Okay. Forgive me, but I have to know. When was the last time?"

"Oh, sweet God, it's been ages. Maybe a month, maybe two."

"And so what did he do?"

"He sat in his chair, drank his coffee, read his newspaper, did the crossword puzzle. And didn't even bother to look at me."

Carmela slapped her hands on the chair. "Didn't I tell you? Something's going on—yes or no?"

"He's sixty-four years old, for Chrissake! Don't you think that has something to do with it?"

"Like hell. I'm fifty-one and I want it all the time. If only I had a good man to do it with! No, I'm sorry. I've known plenty of men that age with perfectly healthy appetites. Older, even! And they don't have Bluhm's playground history. It's what I told you, Maria. He's getting it somewhere else!"

"From whom?"

"I don't know! Maybe you're right to worry about your maid. The most dangerous women come in the most unexpected packages. But I'd wager that if he's going after her, she's not the only one. How can you be sure what goes on in that appliance store, eh? Do you know who he's spending time with on his lunch hour?"

"No."

"Well, you'd better find out!"

Maria's hands flew to her mouth. "I have nowhere to go if he throws me out," she whispered.

"You listen to me," Carmela said, "and I swear: You'll stay in this house for as long as your little heart desires."

"How?"

Carmela heaved herself out of the chair good-naturedly and lumbered toward the door, where she had deposited a bright green bag of woven straw. She hoisted it up and lugged it toward the bed, wobbling precariously on her shoes. "I've been doing a bit of research, hon. We're going to fix you up. We're going to go at him the way a bullfighter goes at a bull."

She dropped the bag on the bed and drew out a number of string-tied parcels, placing them on the bedspread carefully. Maria approached, tantalized. There were bundles great and small, tied with different colors, labeled in a tiny but careful hand. She could see only a few words here and there as Carmela organized them into piles: One packet was labeled LILAC and, under that, the word PILLOW; another said LICORICE and, below it, FOOTPRINTS. There were more than twenty and, as Carmela began to unwrap them, checking the contents against a tidily folded list, Maria marveled at what she saw. There were candles of many hues, long wands of incense, bags filled with damp seaweed, diminutive bottles of oil, vials of powders, a jar of dried roots. Finally Carmela pulled out two gilded frames, displaying the likenesses of saints.

"Magic?" Maria said, in wonder. "You're proposing black magic?"

"Oh, I wouldn't go so far as to say that. We're just going to put a little spell on Mr. Bluhm."

"What kind?"

"The binding kind. To keep him faithful." She paused to let this proposition sink in. "I wish to God I'd tried this on Willy when he showed signs of drifting...when he began feeling sorry for his wife. I tried every trick I could think of! Dolls, pins, chicken hearts, you name it! But once a man makes up his mind, what can you do?" She shrugged and leaned back against the headboard. "That's my sad story. But, as for you," she sighed, "you still have time." She reached out and patted her hand. "Listen. It's all very simple." She sat up and grabbed two little bags eagerly. "You're going to sew crushed flowers into his pillow. Each day, when he goes off to work, you're going to sprinkle some powder in his tracks. Somehow, you'll have to figure out a way to dab his forehead with oil. You'll need to hide this picture of St. Peter by the front door and this of St. Michael by the back, bury a little seaweed in the garden, burn some candles, and get him to swallow two tablespoons of *chamico* every day."

"Where did you get all this?" Maria felt a flicker of hope now, for if she had ever believed in anything, it was in the power to enhance and redress fortune. The amulets she had directed at Bluhm when she was a girl were ample proof of that. They had worked. But she had gotten cocky and over-confident; she'd abandoned such things long ago.

"There's a shop I go to in Breña. I asked my friend there to recommend the ingredients. She gave me all this and told me exactly what to do."

And so the women began to plan, in the most detailed manner, how to prevent Bluhm from straying. That very evening, Maria would stir two heaping tablespoons of *chamico*—a strong jungle herb—into his fried beans; the next, it would be blended into his chowder. She would need to bathe her breasts and thighs each night with a rosemary infusion and slip a few drops of that old bathwater into his morning coffee. She would have to bury a clump of seaweed just inside the front gate—below the last bit of dirt he would tread before stepping out into the wider world. And there were more rituals, many more, to do.

The next morning, when Bluhm went off to work, Maria sprinkled licorice powder on his footprints. She hid St. Peter behind a cactus that flanked the front door and St. Michael beneath the garlic pot in the kitchen window. She set the flask of linden oil on the hall table so that she would remember to dab some on Bluhm's forehead before bedtime. All day she burned incense at the foot of his bed and candles at the foot of hers. She improvised a shrine from one of his old photographs. With only an hour to go before he returned from work, she was hurrying to sew dried lilac blossoms into Bluhm's pillow when she heard a rustle, glanced up, and saw Flavia standing in the doorway. The maid had a bewildered look on her face. She had watched Maria disgorge and restuff the master's pillow and was struggling to comprehend what she had seen.

"Why are you standing there with your trap wide open?"
Maria demanded.

Flavia blinked and stepped back, pulling at her own fingers.

"Answer!"

"I . . . I was just coming to . . . I didn't expect to find you
here, señora."

"You didn't expect to find me in my own house? In my own
husband's bedroom?"

Flavia knew very well that Bluhm wasn't Maria's husband,
but she didn't dare say so. She stared down at her shoes.

"This is my house, understand? You should expect to find
me anywhere in it, especially in this room. Now, get out!"

"Yes, señora." The girl backed out swiftly and closed the
door.

There was still much to do. How to stir more herbs into his
dinner without stirring them into everyone else's? Carmela
hadn't said what would happen if Maria and Flavia were to in-
gest the concoction. She had to mix a bath of sea salt and
rosemary and hide it somehow so that she could bathe in it for
nine days in a row before flinging it toward the sunrise. These
things needed to be attended to meticulously. On the ninth
day, the spell would be complete.

Maria couldn't remember when she had been so engaged,
so resourceful. Perhaps it was years of accumulated fear that
someday Bluhm would exile her from that sanctuary. Or the
conviction that she had a right to the house—that twenty
years had bought a legitimate foothold to his property. She
had worked hard to win his trust, and she had prevailed,

despite all their differences. There was no doubt that he had once loved her. She recalled how he would run a finger along her spine to signal his desire, how he would cradle her against the night, kiss her hands. Maybe it was too late to revive that love, too late to persuade him to marry. But she'd be damned before she'd let another woman take him away.

THE CONVERSATION AT THE BAR had started Bluhm thinking—when had he become such a stranger to his own friends? Was he such a puzzle that they needed to sit there and hash out his motives? Marco had been wrong—it wasn't Maria's race that kept Bluhm from the altar. And yet Willy hadn't been altogether right either.

Perhaps it was just time. Accumulated time. The more of it that passed, the less urgency he felt. What was so wrong with leaving well enough alone?

At the very beginning, when Maria had first moved in, he had been startled by the hostility from his friends, his neighbors, his business associates, mere strangers on the street. Even pure-blooded Indians seemed taken aback or offended to see a white man arm in arm with a girl of their own color. He was made to feel wrong, depraved. How often had he been taken aside at the door of a fancy establishment and told that his whore couldn't come inside?

He had fought those battles, sometimes with his fists. There was something physically thrilling about it, especially afterward, when she would repay his chivalry between the sheets. It didn't matter that business was bad, that cameras were totally beside the point now, that Shining Path rebels were marauding the streets, terrorizing the city. They had a world in which to tend their love. Somehow, they managed to eat. And somehow, with time, he learned to weather the stares, pretend he didn't hear when passersby growled, *"Gringo cholero!"* Indian fucker.

Back then everything seemed out of control, the whole country in dire need of a more temperate nature. Three months after Maria came to live with him, the terrorists warned they would mark the anniversary of the prison massacre with a show of terrible force. "Blood will run!" a terrorist cell announced from its base in Miraflores. That day passed uneventfully, but just before sunset, Bluhm's doorbell rang and, when he went to see who it was, he found himself face to face with a tiny rag of a woman, supported at the elbow by a boy no older than Fritz. She was agitated and trembling; he, sweating, malodorous. Bluhm took them for a pair of belligerents and was just about to summon the street-corner soldier, when the youth blurted the name: "Maria Fernandez."

"What about her?" Bluhm said.

"This is her mother," the young man responded. "I am her brother Pablo."

He let them into his garden, alarmed that Maria was kin to such blighted, repellent people. The sick woman sucked on a loose tooth, weaving back and forth as she took his measure. The boy was scrawny, sullen, his sparse beard scarcely masking his chin.

Pablito explained why they were there. Their neighbors in

Lurigancho were deathly afraid of the anniversary of the prison massacre, he said. They were fleeing their homes and abandoning what little they had, fearing the revenge that was sure to follow. A week before, Freddy had gone off into the hills with a band of insurgents and now, without him, the frail woman felt unmoored and vulnerable. They had nowhere else to go.

They stayed for a month out in the servants' quarters, although nothing like a bloodbath in Lurigancho ever happened—only the car bombs, the damaged pylons, the infuriating blackouts that continued to afflict the city. Pablito tended the garden, hosed down the driveway, swept the floors. Maria waited on her mother, darting around the kitchen, making bean cakes and fortified soups. Anyone could see it was a time of joy for Maria, but it was a time of reckoning for Bluhm, for if he ever believed he was free of racism—that he was a man, as Willy had put it, with "an absolute lack of prejudice"—he would be disabused of that notion now. He found Berta Fernandez repulsive, her high cackle lewd and jarring; and, as much as Pablito was trying to be useful, he struck Bluhm as sulky and ill-tempered, wandering the house like a feral dog.

There was nothing in their faces, their carriage, or their manner that seemed remotely related to the girl. And there was the matter of their smell: an unmistakably acrid odor that emanated from their mouths and hair. Maria, too, seemed altered by their presence. She was louder, coarser, chewing her food with her mouth open, devouring her meals with her elbows on her knees. She was always with them, and at night when he trudged up the stairs alone, he would hear them in the kitchen, howling like a coven of jackals. Once, when he came home from work, late and exhausted, he was surprised not to hear them at all. He tiptoed to the kitchen, pushed open the door, and there they were, huddled around the table, sucking on chicken feet, looking up as if he were an intruder in his own house.

That was when he resolved that he'd had enough. For all Maria's tears and implorations, he told them they had to go.

Bluhm remembered all this as he contemplated Willy's words about his lack of racism. He recalled the dread that possessed him throughout that endless month: that his precious house would now fall into the hands of the washerwoman. But Berta Fernandez died shortly after she went back to Lurigancho, and Pablito drifted away, perfectly capable of feeding himself. There was no one to lay claims, when all was said and done, but Maria. And still, he was unwilling to give her what she so clearly desired. Why?

Bluhm came and went from work in the next few days, worried about this—sure that his friend had spoken of him too generously—feeling woozy and out of sorts. He found himself fretting like an old man about his physical well-being. There was something distinctly wrong with his sinuses. His tongue. His coffee was suddenly acidic. His food had a slightly burned tang to it, the sauces were a little bitter—and yet, when he complained to Maria, she insisted that her food was fine. Even his sense of smell, which had always been exceptional, seemed to play tricks on him. He could have sworn he smelled anise in the garden, although nothing like that had ever grown there. He detected the slightest hint of sandal-wood too, whenever he opened the door to his room. But the strangest thing was that all night long he was tormented by the scent of his mother's lilacs. He would fall asleep with the sensation that he was surrounded by them. He would wake up with their aroma still lingering in his head. And yet his mother's lilacs no longer grew in the garden. They hadn't been there in years. They had been ravaged by mold, cut down, and burned long ago, shortly after his mother died.

SHE COULD SEE THAT THE SPELL was taking effect. He was feeling its physical impact now. Every night after they ate, he would ask her to place a hand on his forehead and try to detect the fever. His body heat was always the same, always normal, but it gave her an opportunity to dab on a little linden oil and lead him away to bed.

Once there, she would knead his legs with the essence of bitter oranges. She would rub bay rum on the back of his neck. After he had relaxed and surrendered to her ministrations, she would undress in the dark and crawl under the sheets with him. There was something heartbreaking about the large, pale man submitting to her so sweetly. In earlier years he had been the assertive one, always first to show his desire. But during these last seven days of the spell, even as he fretted and fussed that he was not altogether well, it was she who took his manhood as if it were a sleeping animal, and he who received her gratefully on his back. "I want you so much," he'd whisper. "So very much right now." Afterward, she would cradle him in her arms until he fell to breathing heavily, and then she would slip off to bathe in the rosemary water and burn candles before her shrine.

"In the heat of sex, we are a single race," her old friend Monica would say as the dancers crowded around the cracked mirror at Lima Nights, putting on lipstick, fluffing their hair. Certainly, for Bluhm and Maria, it had been true. Even with all their differences—all the ways they were reminded that two human beings couldn't possibly be more dissimilar—in the act of sex there was but one language, one story, one synchronized arc of rapture. In the heat of sex, they were exactly the same.

Squatting in the small washtub she had hidden in her bathroom, washing the fragrant water over her for the seventh time, Maria recalled the first time she had ever turned Bluhm away. It was only a few weeks after she had moved in with him. They had been in the kitchen at dusk on a Sunday—she peeling hot, boiled potatoes, he hunting through the phone book for merchants of used furniture—when they heard a gentle rustling in the garden. Bluhm had gone to the window, pulled back the shade, and peered into the gloom of early evening. Suddenly and wordlessly, he bolted out of the room.

She wiped her hands on a rag and ran after, but when she got as far as the hall, she heard him outside talking to someone. There were, in fact, three distinct male voices beyond the massive front wall, but the speakers could not be seen from any of the windows. She ran upstairs to the veranda, where she saw them out there in the twilight. Bluhm and his two sons. The taller one, Fritz, whom she barely recognized, had a restraining hand on the shoulder of the younger one. Bluhm was speaking passionately to the boy, his hands palm up, in entreaty. The boy couldn't have been much older than she was, and she saw instinctively that he was not himself—that the pain of holding back tears was excruciating. His brow was furrowed, his face flushed, his eyes stormy. He was grabbing at air furiously, trying to get his hands on his father, but Fritz was clutching him fast, imploring him to calm down.

All at once, the boy glanced up and saw her. He drew back his arms and straightened. And then his face went slack, as if he were receiving, not imparting, emotion now—comprehending something for the first time. The two of them studied each other while Bluhm continued to speak, oblivious. The boy was smaller and slighter than the other two, but his shoulders were strong and square, his features handsome, hair the color of corn.

He looked at her with the alert, watchful gaze of one animal appraising another. They held that gaze as Bluhm spoke, as Fritz listened to his father intently, as dusk deepened and neighboring houses winked to life, one by one. She could not help but sense that the person she saw there—so full of passion at one moment, so full of vigilance the next—was Bluhm himself as a much younger man. In any case, this strange white boy with the radiant hair and angry eyes was a part of Bluhm she didn't know, would never know.

That night, when Bluhm reached across the bed to take her in his arms, she could not bring herself to make love. She pretended to be fast asleep.

. . .

BLUHM WAS FEELING MORE PECULIAR by the day. Apart from the smells and tastes, his hearing, too, seemed afflicted. When the radio alarm went off, giving him the brisk, first news of morning, he could hardly hear it. He was finding it all too easy to sleep in far later than he should, luxuriating in the bower of his mother's lilacs. Some mornings he was barely making it to Hiraoka before the store threw open its doors.

But, in other ways, his physical prowess had improved. Maria was coming to his bed every night now. On the rare occasions they had made love in recent years, it usually had been he who crept through the dark, hoping to stir her to former passions. But suddenly she was insatiable, slipping her sweet nakedness under his covers, putting her clever hands on all the right places, using her pretty pink tongue to tease and delight him in ways he had forgotten possible. His body was as virile as it had ever been, his sex as hard as a spear. What new hormone was traveling his arteries? What new factor had turned the tide? How, in this sixty-fifth year of mortality, could he last so long into the night?

Every day after work and before dinner, he would contemplate this new state in the solitude of his study as Maria flitted about the house, occupying herself with a dozen chores—doing God knew what. He would take that moment of peace to browse through newsletters from the Club Germania and read about the Mozart competition, an upcoming pilsner night for Oktoberfest, the latest group trip to Bavaria. All that Teutonic mirth! It brought him close to nostalgia. From time to time he would listen to music. He had tried to fill Rudy's absence by buying—on staff discount—a high-quality audio system. He had built an impressive CD collection, made up entirely of German composers, in mournful works featuring the cello. On Sundays after lunch, he would slip Yo-Yo Ma's recording of *"Erbarme Dich"* into his machine, sit back, and reflect on that world gone by.

The last time he had heard Rudy play the cello was at a concert nineteen years before, two days before the boy's graduation from the Humboldt School. It was a sunny day in December, and the student orchestra was performing outside by the shallow pool in the school's garden. There were ten rows of folding chairs, perched unevenly on pavement and grass, and the audience sat with their backs to Avenida Benavides, buffering the hum of traffic. Bluhm had seen Sophie in the distance and, following their custom of strict separation, he was careful to take a seat far from the palm tree under which she was standing. But the moment he sat down, he glanced over and caught her eye. She was thinner than she'd ever been, hair pulled back tight, face gaunt and haggard. He had sensed from the unruffled way she was looking at him that she wanted to talk, but he couldn't bring himself to approach her. There was something unnerving in that stare: aloof, ever accusatory, but lacking the edge of rancor to which he had grown accustomed. An infinite sadness lived in those eyes. He often wondered, after Sophie died, what she would have said had he had the courage to walk over and speak to her.

After the concert, Bluhm had taken Rudy to a modest restaurant on the other side of the avenue—a visit Sophie had approved since Bluhm had indicated he would not attend the Westermanns' graduation party. Father and son took a table at the rear of the place and ordered two thick *butifarras*—sandwiches of pork with lettuce and a tart onion sauce. Rudy was polite but hardly the lighthearted, whimsical boy he had been before the separation. Bluhm hadn't seen that sunny boy since the day he had packed him off to the beach the summer before. The night the boys had slipped into the garden, Bluhm had tried to explain that he would always love them deeply but it was too late to recover his marriage to Sophie. Too much damage had been done. When Fritz finally took his brother away, Rudy was visibly shaken. He had never been the same again, and Bluhm was forced to admit that the distant boy sitting across the table was the one he himself had made.

Once the meal was finished, Bluhm tried to stretch time by dawdling over a cup of coffee. Before long, Rudy looked up with his sea-green eyes and said simply, "She's really something, isn't she, Pa?" When Bluhm asked what he meant, Rudy explained that he had caught a glimpse of Maria that night, a little more than a year before, with her long ebony hair draped over her shoulders and her black eyes bright with tears. She was, he said, the most beautiful girl he had ever seen.

They never talked about her again, and Bluhm doubted that Rudy ever laid eyes on her after that brief interlude. But he had always wondered why Maria hadn't mentioned that she had seen his sons from the veranda, and he pondered why, after all the shouting, he had come in to find her deep under covers, still as stone.

He was mulling those random memories, listening to Casals's cello soar through the intricate cadences of a Schumann trio, when the door to the study opened and he saw Flavia's pale little face come into view. He reached for the remote control and turned off the music. "Dinner?" he said genially. "Is it ready?"

To his surprise she came in, closed the door, and whispered loudly for him to turn on the music again. The behavior was odd, possibly impertinent, but he had always liked the girl and did as she said. Casals was suddenly back in the room, pouring his soul into the trio's wistful third movement. Flavia gave Bluhm·a grateful smile and stepped forward tentatively, working her apron with her hands. She started to speak, but it was impossible to hear her. He lowered the volume. "What, what? Speak up. I can't hear a word."

She came closer, staring at her feet, until she was so near he could smell her. It pleased him to think his faculties hadn't disappeared altogether. She was exuding a distinct, not unpleasant aroma of onions, celery, and cilantro. What was it they were having for dinner, then? He contemplated it with greater interest now. Fish? No, he would have smelled that. Beef? He would have detected that too. Ah, it was probably chicken.

"I don't want the señora to hear," she said, after glancing repeatedly at the door.

"Oh? And what could you possibly have to tell me that she can't be told too?"

"I'm worried about your health, señor. I've heard you complaining to the señora that you don't feel well, and I think I know what's wrong."

He was caught short by this. He had not thought she was the kind of servant to assert her opinions. He had tried often to jolly and cajole her when he passed through the kitchen, let her know that she didn't have to creep through his house, afraid. But he had not expected her to respond by barging in and giving him medical advice—and, to top it off, behind Maria's back.

But she seemed genuinely anxious. "Well, well. Don't just stand there. Tell me what's wrong, then."

"It's a hex, señor," she whispered, the words hissing through the music. "They're putting a hex on you. With herbs! Potions! Black witchery! I've seen the evidence myself."

He was so unprepared for the kitchen girl's diagnosis he couldn't think what to say. Casals's breathtaking cadenza, sundering the air with its wild virtuosity, was the only reply.

She sighed and her thin shoulders dropped in abject resignation. "I was afraid you wouldn't believe me," she said.

He half-laughed, half-snorted. "Where do I begin, Flavia? Let's start with this, shall we? Who is 'they'?"

"The señora and her fat friend."

Bluhm was even more taken aback. He hadn't seen Carmela in the house for a blessedly long time now. He'd assumed that Maria had finally seen the light. But more disturbing, Flavia was attacking her own mistress. Who did she think she was to disparage the lady of the house so freely? The insolence!

"Flavia, I suggest you go back to your room and think about what you've just said. Hex? Black witchery? Where in the world did you get those ridiculous notions? Let's get one thing straight—I'm German. You know anything about Germans?" She looked at him blankly. "You hear that music? *That's* German!" He tapped a forefinger to his head in time to the music. "*Ein, zwei, drei!* We are orderly, precise people. We don't believe in that jungle claptrap. And we don't put up with domestics who don't understand their place in a house."

Schumann's finale came to a vibrant climax, as if to punctuate Bluhm's censure. The girl opened her mouth to speak—Bluhm didn't know whether she would now make excuses, argue her point, or apologize—but suddenly they both heard Maria's voice reverberating through the house, growing louder.

"Flavia! Where are you? And where in God's name is dinner? Get yourself in the kitchen, now!"

The maid spun on her heels and ran, slamming the door behind her.

7

Barbs

TERCIO DE BANDILLERAS

WHAT WAS THAT SKINNY LITTLE WOMAN DOING IN his study? Just when she should have been putting food on the table? Maria had seen Flavia dart from Bluhm's sanctuary. The door opened and shut, exposing her in a quick flicker of light, and then all Maria saw was a shadow, slipping through the dark like a bad omen.

Carmela was right. Though Flavia was a nobody, an ugly little thing, it didn't mean she couldn't have designs on the man of the house. What was it Carmela had said, exactly? "The most dangerous women come in the most unexpected packages"? How true it was. Mrs. Bluhm had probably never imagined that one day she would lose her husband to a fifteen-year-old girl at the neighborhood supermarket. Maria might even have helped her through the checkout line, stuffed her bags, smiled good-bye. Off she had gone, without so much as a backward glance. If Bluhm could go from white to brown, he could go from bargirl to scullery maid, upstairs to down. Men were that way. Especially if women pandered to them.

But that had to stop—here, now, in this house. She had been lax in tending the fires of his love, but she would not be so inattentive now. She would change the order of things. She would reverse this tide.

"What was Flavia doing in your study?" Maria asked Bluhm later that night as she rubbed his back with essence of verbena. He was naked, facedown, helpless. A string of saliva dropped indolently from his mouth, spreading its wetness onto the pillow. He stirred slightly and opened his eyes.

"Calling me to dinner."

"With the door closed?" Maria purred, trying not to sound in the least accusatory.

"Was it closed? I didn't notice."

She kept working his shoulder blades, running her fingers along his spine, lightening the pressure until she reached the swell of his buttocks. She was straddling his thighs and slipped now toward his knees.

"So, you were watching?" he said suddenly, lifting and turning his head, but not enough to meet her eyes. His hair was mussed, the bald spot on top glinting with oil.

"No! What do you mean?"

"I mean—how do you know the door was closed unless you were standing there watching?"

Maria hesitated. What was he up to? Why was he quizzing her on what *she'd* been doing—shifting the suspicion to her? She was on the verge of flinging the sheet in his face and stalking back to her room, but she closed her eyes and concentrated on her objective. What good were these last eight days—to what end would she have worked this spell—only to throw it all over and abandon it now? She shook more liquid onto her hands, rubbed her palms vigorously, and worked to summon the memory of her former life: the dust, the grit, the grinding hunger. "I wasn't watching the door, darling. I just happened by, wondering why dinner wasn't on the table."

"Oh."

When she was finished, she made love to him. Then she switched off the light and crawled in beside him, pulling the sheet over them like a cocoon. But for all her assiduousness that night, for all her attention to his pleasure, he seemed a bit subdued. And for all his sweetness, and for all his applied, accumulated knowledge of her body, she couldn't get her mind off the maid.

When morning came, she waited until Bluhm was gone before she dragged the washtub of nine-day-old rosemary water to the head of the staircase so that she could carry it downstairs. But she barely got it through the door and into the hallway when she realized that she would never be able to manage it alone. Grudgingly, she called down to Flavia, and the girl instantly scampered up the stairs, brushing the hair from her face.

"Help me carry this down to the garden," Maria commanded.

Flavia looked down at the cloudy water, her face a mask of bewilderment. "But, señora," she said, "why don't we just empty this into a bathtub up here?"

"Do as I say."

"All the way to the garden?"

"Yes! The garden!" She screamed it so loudly, the girl shrank back, afraid. "Don't ask so many questions, for God's sake," Maria cried, exasperated. "Just pick up your side! Do it!"

They struggled with the unwieldy tub, wrestling it this way and that, as the contents sloshed over the rim. Grunting, panting, sliding on the wet wood, they staggered down the long staircase, set it down briefly, and then lugged it all the way out to the front path. Maria could see she was being watched: A neighbor stared at her from a passing car; a guard at the embassy residence cocked his head.

Carmela's instructions had specified this step in the enchantment should come just after dawn, not at nine in the morning, but the sun was not high and it was easy to see in what direction she needed to hurl the bathwater. "I'm going to stand with my back to the sun," she told Flavia, "and you're going to stand there, facing it. We're going to lift this water high, then toss it over my left shoulder."

To her surprise, the girl did not question it. She dutifully raised her end of the tub and then gave the whole thing a good heave so that it flew over Maria's shoulder and crashed to the ground, splashing rosemary and saltwater on the already yellowed hosta. The faces in the street registered surprise.

Maria paid no attention. She bent down to wipe the moisture from her bare legs. The back of her skirt was drenched. Flavia emptied the remaining water from the tub, then dragged it toward the slate walk. "Was that magic, señora?" she finally asked.

"What's it to you?" Maria snapped.

"Nothing! Please forgive me. I don't mean to meddle! It's just that it seemed to me that that's what it was." She attempted a conspiratorial grin.

Maria wondered whether she should fire the miserable girl on the spot. Didn't she understand that the only thing worse than an insolent maid was a too-friendly one? But Bluhm would be furious. He had hired Flavia himself, as an indulgence. And indeed, the girl had made Maria's life easier: For three full years now, Maria no longer had to scrub floors, do laundry, cook. But it was a double-edged sword, this business of servants—in every way, a nettlesome complication.

Maria sighed. "I'm having a little fun, Flavia. That's all. Just don't get in my way, okay?" She clapped the water from her hands and went inside.

BLUHM LAY IN BED, contemplating the fissures in his ceiling. Maria had stayed long into the night and, as he'd slipped in and out of perplexing dreams, he had felt her there, radiating heat, shifting fitfully. When he'd awakened in the predawn, she was still there, her fragrance of apples filling his senses. But when light came and the day's news began to blare at him from the clock radio, he rubbed his eyes and she was gone.

There had been nights, just after she'd moved into her own room, that he longed for that restless human presence: the small foot hooked over his heel; the light arm flung across his chest; the long black hair over his face, blocking the day. But time and age had made inevitable realignments. The small foot, like all the rest of her, had grown heavier; the flung arm, an irritation; the long black hair, bleached and shorn. Little by little, he'd learned to prize the solitude. There was something unarguably welcome in the ability to turn on a light, move around the room whenever he wanted to: a slight but precious freedom of the will.

Why was she suddenly so attentive? Why all the tenderness and care? His eyes followed the cracks in the yellowed plaster, wandering from wall to wall and back again. The whole room needed a good painting—had for a long time—but there had been more-pressing obligations. More-urgent demands. All at once, his eyes lit on a shadow just below the molding, a small aberration above the door. At first, he thought it was a rut in the plaster, easily enough patched. But when he focused more sharply, he could see it was convex, not concave—a diminutive object hanging just above the frame, poised precariously on the narrow lip of wood.

He sat up, trying to get a better look, but still couldn't make out what it was. He dragged a chair to the door, clambered on, but not until he stood on his toes and stretched his arm high was he able to touch it. The thing was fixed somehow, and soft; he gave a little tug and it came away readily into his hand.

He stepped down and inspected it closely. It was a gray velvet pouch, drawn shut with a string—so light it had been secured to the wood with ordinary tape. He pulled it open and drew out a glass vial, no longer than his little finger. Inside was a blackened scrap of gauze. He removed the tiny stopper, hoping to get at the contents, but the mouth of the vial was too small. Bringing it toward his nose, he detected a sharp, ferric odor—as bracing as a darkroom chemical.

He was about to take it to Maria to share his bizarre discovery, but something held him back. He sat on the bed and thought about what Flavia had said. Was the vial some kind of talisman? Was it the black witchery she had seen—the thing she had taken as evidence?

"Your breakfast, señor?" Flavia said agreeably when he burst into the kitchen, still buttoning his shirt.

"No, no." This time it was he who came in and closed the door. He took the gray pouch from his pocket and dangled it in front of her face. "Is this it? Is this what you saw?"

She frowned. "What is it?"

"I don't know! That's why I'm asking you. It was in my room, taped above the door."

She dropped her dishrag, hands flying to her mouth.

"I see," he said. "I see."

In truth, he didn't see much of anything at all. He had no idea what he was holding, no notion why it had been hung in his room. Of course, if anyone was capable of planting a talisman, it was Maria. He remembered her carrying those infernal amulets all the time, worrying them like a child. But this secret vial was troubling. Especially inasmuch as everything about her seemed highly erratic lately. Erratic, and wonderful, and strange.

That morning at work, as he put inventory on the shelves and reviewed the latest manuals, the vial gnawed at him, pushing itself into his thoughts. He took it in and out of his coat pocket numerous times, filling his nasal passages with its acrid, oddly familiar aroma. By noon he was on the phone, asking Willy to meet him at the Café Haiti.

Bluhm left work promptly at six and headed directly for the Parque Kennedy. As he crossed the street and followed the rim of the park, he could see Willy's familiar profile bent over an outdoor table at the Haiti, his back to the looming gray church. He was reading a book, smoking, and scratching his head. Bluhm was so eager for his advice that, even as he pulled out a chair and sat down, he was telling Willy about the maid, the pouch, and the glass vial. Before long, he pulled the mysterious object from his pocket and passed it to his friend.

Willy stubbed out his cigarette and turned the eerie little flask over in his hands, contemplating the stained cloth inside. When he was done, he shoved it back into the gray bag and pushed it across the table. "My guess is your maid's right. It's voodoo. Carmela was always going to those shops, snooping around. It scared me shitless."

"What do I do? Confront Maria?"

"Absolutely not," said Willy. "Go to the best *vidente*—the best seer—you can find. You have to fight fire with fire, go mano a mano with the woman. Show him this thing, ask him what kind of magic it is. That way you'll know what she's up to. Otherwise, she can say anything she wants and you'll never know what her real motives are."

Bluhm laughed, half at the ridiculousness of his situation, half out of utter despair. "I can't believe it, Brenner! Here you are talking about real *motives*. You seriously think she would want to harm me?"

"Yes, Bluhm. Don't you remember when Carmela broke into my house? Flooded my living room with a garden hose? We still have the watermarks on the walls. She stalked Beatriz all around Lima, frightening the daylights out of her. She kept calling the house again and again, playing a cassette of love songs I'd once given her. And how about the red paint she smeared on my door?"

"But you left her, Brenner. Maria and I have been under the same roof now for twenty years!"

"She's wanted more than a roof from you, Bluhm. You know it. We've all talked about it. She wants your name. She wants your ring on her finger."

"Putting a hex on me is no way to get it!"

"Of course not. Hey, settle down! Don't get upset. She's doing what she knows. She's an Indian, for Chrissake!"

Their conversation went on for another hour, leaving Bluhm with a combination of ease and dread. Never had he felt he was entering into something so foreign to his nature— so inimical to his pragmatic self. He felt at once foolish and hopeful when, at last, he asked Willy, "So, do you know any *videntes?*"

"No, but a secretary in my office is very knowledgeable. Let me ask her; I'll call you tomorrow with her recommendations."

The next morning Willy called Bluhm at work with a name and address. The *vidente* was known only as "Señor Juan" and practiced out of an abandoned shop in a run-down quarter of San Miguel. "He's the most sought-after seer in all Lima!" Willy assured him. "You're in good hands, Bluhm. Believe me, it wasn't easy, but my friend managed to get you an appointment for the day after tomorrow. At ten in the morning. It won't be on German time, though. Be prepared to wait."

"WHAT DO YOU MEAN you can't find it?"

"I can't find it! It's gone—understand? Vanished!" Maria was sitting at her vanity, clutching her head in her hands. Carmela was propped against the bed's headboard, thinking hard.

"Maybe it was the maid," she said at long last. "Did you talk to her?"

"I asked whether she'd taken down a little gray bag—or perhaps found it on the floor. All she did was look at me with that imbecile face of hers and shake her head no."

"So Bluhm must have it."

"I guess so."

"It's not the worst that could happen, Maria. It won't weaken the spell. If anything, it might make it stronger. If the cloth is in his hands, maybe even in his pocket, he'll be more susceptible. Who knows?"

Carmela left not long after that, giving Maria more than an hour to collect herself before Bluhm was expected home. She had been feeling despondent and unsure of herself all day. The directions Carmela had given her initially—spelled out on a sheet of paper and numbered—had been very clear. She was to take the little glass nub down after the ninth day and bury it deep in the garden, in a spot that would be visible from

Bluhm's bedroom window. How could having it suddenly abroad, moving about, possibly on his person, be anything remotely akin to that? How could it make the spell stronger?

All Maria knew was that she could afford no mistakes. She had no one left to go home to in that dung heap of Lurigancho. She had nothing of her own. Everything in Bluhm's little empire, every stick of furniture, every article of her clothing, even the shoes she would be made to walk away in, were bought and paid for by him, owned by him. His.

At the beginning of her spell, she had noted a genuine response to her attentions. He seemed grateful, surprised, even loving in return. But everything was unraveling quickly now: The closed-door conferences with the maid, the missing talisman, the way he had run from the house that morning, the way he was late now in coming home. The universe had shifted. She felt it in her bones.

Bluhm arrived a few minutes before his scheduled appointment. The storefront looked closed, its corrugated aluminum barrier pulled down to the pavement. But when he bent to peek in the small metal door, he could see it was open for business. Three sofas were pushed up against the walls, all of them filled with customers. In the far corner was a glass case lined with colorful bottles of Florida Water. He inhaled, anticipating a pleasant whiff of bergamot and jasmine, but all he could smell was mold.

His first impulse was to flee, but just as he was factoring

that possibility, a plump, friendly woman with a toothy smile and a red scarf appeared, holding a frayed notebook in her hands. She confirmed his name politely, explaining that the others had made no formal appointments. They were there because they hoped to be squeezed in, charged less. Bluhm took a seat on the dingy green sofa and looked around at his fellow supplicants.

A gnomelike man with a black goatee perched on a chair like a crow. A mountain Indian in a colorful shawl was twisting her hair into a braid. A portly matron cradled a sleeping girl. A large man in a bulky gray coat clung to a well-worn book. As Bluhm glanced at the other faces, he was struck by the many walks of life they represented, but except for the television mounted on the wall, its mute images dancing wildly, the room seemed eerily devoid of animation. The walls were equally blank, except for a wooden crucifix over the doorway that led, Bluhm presumed, to Señor Juan himself. A brisk wind swept in under the barrier, chilling the musty air. All at once, a tall woman with bright hair emerged from the dark corridor behind the doorway. Her eyes were black and wide, as if she had just been granted sight. "For God's sake, Tito, let's go," she rasped, clutching the fat beads around her throat. The man in gray hurried forward to meet her. Together, they hunched through the door and disappeared into the windy morning.

The woman in the red scarf reappeared in the hall and beckoned Bluhm forward. The *vidente* was tired, she told him, exhausted by his last customer. He would need to rest and refresh his spirits.

Eleven o'clock came and went, and still Bluhm continued to sit in limbo. Staring at the senseless mayhem on the small screen above him, he began to wonder if he shouldn't have asked his manager for the whole day off instead of just the morning. He should have listened to Willy, who'd warned about delays. Fidgeting with the coins in his pocket, drumming his fingers on his knee, he had little to do as the seer of fortunes slept.

When he was finally admitted, close to noon, the *vidente* seemed vigorous and fresh—the very picture of vitality. Bluhm was expecting a wizened old man, but Señor Juan was young, certainly no older than forty. A light mulatto with close-cropped hair and a barrel chest, he didn't have the slightest air of mystery. He was almond-eyed, smiling, his round face full of welcome. Bluhm shook his hand warmly, immediately comfortable in his presence, marveling at the ordinariness of the man. Señor Juan led him toward a closed door and, swinging it open, guided him into the Stygian darkness.

The room seemed utterly black at first, but even as Bluhm surrendered himself to blindness, he began to see glimmers of light—tiny flames, like infinitesimal stars, dancing in the distance. When his eyes adjusted, he saw it was candlelight: tongues of fire that seemed to multiply miraculously, until there were a dozen or more floating before him, then suddenly, under them, a large wooden table and two chairs.

Señor Juan put Bluhm's hands on the back of one chair, instructed him to sit, and then did the same.

"Your full name," Señor Juan began, placing his fists purposefully on the table.

"Carlos Bluhm von Roedenbeck."

The *vidente* repeated it carefully, syllable by syllable. Then he asked for Bluhm's birth date.

With that portal to Bluhm's identity established, the session was under way. "Why have you come, Carlos Bluhm von Roedenbeck?"

"I would show you, señor, but for the dark in this room."

"You mean the little glass bottle in your pocket?"

Bluhm's tongue froze.

"The bottle with the scrap of cloth inside?" the *vidente* added calmly.

"Yes."

"A woman's menstrual fluid, preserved on a sliver of fabric. Is it cotton? Or is it an artificial fabric? No, no. It's cotton," he said with authority now. "The kind hospitals use on wounds." He was tapping the table with his fingers, his palms flat against the wood. Bluhm sensed a sharp cold at the back of his neck. Menstrual fluid? A wave of nausea coursed through his gut.

"What is it for?" Bluhm asked into the darkness. "What's its purpose?"

"The purpose! Let us ask the saints." The *vidente* began to pat the table more deliberately now, chanting the names of saints—Saint Michael, Saint Peter, Santa Rosa, San Martín— asking them to stand forward. "What does it mean, this blood in the pocket of Carlos Bluhm?" There was a moment's silence as the candlelight flickered fitfully, and then the seer began to mumble, "M-m-mali, m-m-mari . . ." He paused. "Maria?" he asked Bluhm, his angelic face entirely visible now.

"Yes." Bluhm's pulse began to race.

"The one whose blood is in the glass. The one who wants to hold on to you at all costs."

"She wants me to marry her."

"And the truth is that you love her."

"No. . . . Yes."

"But she does not love you."

Bluhm was momentarily struck dumb by that declaration. He struggled against its finality, trying to respond.

"Shh!" the *vidente* said. "I hear them now . . . I hear the voices." The *vidente* sat perfectly still, squeezing his eyes shut. Beads of perspiration sprang onto his upper lip and lined his brow. "The women," he said finally.

"Women?"

"So many of them. Who are these women, Carlos Bluhm?"

He was bewildered. "I've had many in my life, señor," he said at long last. Bluhm dropped his head, tears stinging his eyes. He did not know why, but he felt as if his heart would leap up his chest, burst from his mouth whole.

"One of them is the girl Maria."

"She's not a girl anymore."

"I see dead women too, Carlos Bluhm. They have their backs to you. They have turned away. Even in the afterlife."

"I don't know what you mean, señor."

The *vidente* was staring ahead, oblivious, eyes shining. "I see parties, beautiful parties. I see food and drink in a house filled with happiness and laughter."

"My father's house."

"And then there is silence. An abandoned ship. A desert island."

"My house, señor. My house."

"Because of women . . ."

"Yes . . ."

"I see their bodies everywhere. A sea of womanhood. Why?"

"I don't know. I don't—" Bluhm felt as if something inside were breaking. He took a deep breath and suddenly, not far from his right arm, an army of phantoms emerged—springing through the dark one by one until they were all arrayed on the table before him. He focused his eyes and saw through the dancing light that they were figurines—wooden replicas of saints, dozens of them, spread across the wood, with their backs to him. He drew back in his chair. Why were their backs to him? Why had they turned away? His throat was dry, his body perfectly still, until he realized, scanning the murky shadows, that they were turned in reverence, facing a crucifix on the wall.

"I see an old woman," Señor Juan went on. "She is sad but loyal, a guardian angel to you. Is it Dora? And is she dead? It's hard for me to determine, her presence is so real."

Bluhm's hands were shaking now. He pressed his body into the table and felt his heart pound against the wood. "Dorotea," he said. "My mother." He was briefly filled with joy that she was so present. But that feeling vanished with the man's next words.

"She has been angry with you. But she does not curse you as other women have. You have been cursed by women, Mr. Bluhm."

"By my wife."

"By your wife, yes. But by more, many more. Negative thoughts are powerful toxins. And when tongues speak those thoughts, the toxins become curses—as real as cudgels. These curses have weighed heavily on your life."

"Whose curses? Maria's?"

"Perhaps. She is angry. But there is more than one curse on your head now. I see black forces. I see foreign substances in your food, buried objects in your garden, poison. Watch out."

"What can I do to stop it?"

"Take as many fish heads as you have children, put them in a clean cotton bag with the wings, feet, and heart of a freshly slaughtered chicken. Add something you own—a trinket, a shoelace, a photograph. Throw all this out to the sea at sunset, in low tide."

Bluhm drew himself up, incredulous. "I am sorry, señor— fish heads? Chicken parts? It all sounds too strange to me. I don't believe it."

"Believe it."

The *vidente* began to slap the table lightly, chanting the names of more saints—Saint James, Santa Monica, Saint John—interjecting Bluhm's name, and Maria's, and Dorotea's among them. Suddenly he stopped and looked deep into Bluhm's eyes. "Do you have a question for the blessed saints, Carlos Bluhm? They're listening now."

Bluhm thought for a moment and said, "Yes. I want to know what Sophie wanted to say to me that afternoon under the palm tree."

"Your wife?"

Bluhm nodded.

"She wanted to tell you that she was ill, Carlos Bluhm. That she was dying. She didn't know when it would come. She didn't know how much longer she had. But she wanted to say that she knew how much you loved her children. That she was leaving them in good hands. That you had always been a good father to Fritz." The *vidente* stopped there, and Bluhm held his breath. "And to Rudy," Señor Juan finally added.

Bluhm lowered his head and rested it on the table. The wood seemed to breathe beneath him, or perhaps it was merely his imagination. Or was it his own blood, whirling through him like a dark, fierce river?

"That's enough, then," the *vidente* said, patting him on the shoulder. "Enough." He opened Bluhm's hand and put something very small, very cold into it. "Take this stone, Carlos Bluhm. It has listened to you and to me and to all the saints gathered here at this table. Put it in a safe place, close by at all times."

SHE KNEW WHAT IT WAS the moment she saw it. Bluhm was not one to collect lucky stones. But there it was, sitting out on his night table—a lump of shiny black granite. It could mean only one thing: He had found the pouch, gone to a shaman. Now he was answering in kind.

She contemplated calling Carmela but thought better of it. Carmela had gotten her into this fix in the first place. And she didn't want to risk having that woman under his nose any more than she had to. He had made his aversion to Carmela all too clear.

But she had no other friends to turn to. She tried calling Pablito on his cell phone in hopes he might offer some human contact, but he was in the middle of a job, hauling bales off a container ship in Callao. He had no time to talk—and, in any case, he would hardly have been inclined to, had he known the subject she had in mind. As for Flavia: The girl had declared sides. She was no fool. She knew under whose roof she was.

And yet Maria had to admit: The spell had been anything but a failure. Bluhm had been eager in bed, responsive to her advances. If the potions were supposed to encourage him to be faithful, perhaps they had done their work. There was no evidence to the contrary. The problem was that she couldn't be sure. She did not understand Bluhm. She never had. She had no idea what went on in his head, no notion of how his mind worked. What was it the fortune-teller had said? That they were destined, like chicken and goose, to live side by side with no common language—to carry on, clucking and honking, dropping blank eggs into straw?

For years she had taken him for granted, never imagining he might tire of her, banish her, replace her with someone new. But now, suddenly, with her very fate in jeopardy, she needed a way into his soul. Sitting on the veranda, painting her toenails a bright shade of coral, she began to review what she knew of Bluhm. She appreciated by now his propensity for routine—that joyful banging of pots and pans whenever he made his pilsner. His Friday ritual of cleaning the cameras. Or that heartbreaking music he played on Sunday afternoons. She understood that he loved to eat sausages with unpronounceable names, accompanied with great heaps of cold potato or pickled cabbage. She understood, too, that he was a fanatic for neatness: He liked his shirts crisply starched, his room and office dust-free, his fruits unblemished. But what did she know about his heart?

She recalled those early days when his love was much in evidence. He had worried about her welfare then, believing fifteen was too young, when in reality—in the universe from which she had fled—fifteen was a lifetime. She remembered his tenderness that day in Marco's hotel when he had reached for her so hungrily. How happy they had been! He had said sweet words to her, promising he would never hurt her. And then they had taught each other a few things: She told him that tangos filled her with joy and sadness all at once, and he said he felt the same about his son's music. She had said that her favorite dish was a hot, freshly fried *papa rellena,* and he countered with a steaming bowl of sauerkraut, suffused with caraway. When she had told him about amulets and fortune-tellers, he answered with the equivalents in his world: hypnosis, psychology, doctors who could make you see into other people's heads.

Oscar. She put down the nail enamel, screwed the top tight. Why hadn't she thought of it before? Oscar was a psychiatrist. He lived in Bluhm's world. Knew Bluhm. It was Oscar she needed to see: Oscar, who could help her unlock the mysteries of Bluhm's heart. She hardly knew the doctor, had talked to him only once on that night long ago. He had struck her as entirely human—somewhat injured, slightly rattled—not the confident lion he made himself out to be. And he had seemed willing to accept them as a couple; he had been genuinely interested in her.

The more she contemplated it, the more Oscar Weiss seemed to be the answer. He was her way to Bluhm: She had only to seek him out, enlist him. If Bluhm had consulted a shaman, as the black amulet indicated he had, she would consult a German medicine man. She, too, would answer in kind.

THE FISH HEADS AND the freshly slaughtered chicken were easy enough to find, but the personal trinket was harder. He spent much of Saturday afternoon puttering around the house, riffling through drawers, trying to decide what might represent him yet be entirely dispensable. Everywhere he looked, he found things to distract him: a tiny pink shell Maria had rescued from the beach; a terse note in Sophie's immaculate hand, informing him Fritz would graduate with honors. In the end, he opted for one of the photographs Maria had taken of him in the old Peugeot. It felt suitably intimate; still, he could not say he liked the face that leered back from the yellowed paper. It was smug, sophomoric, full of that rude hubris he had come to despise in self-important men. The picture would not be missed.

The trout heads that signified his sons came wrapped in waxed paper, tied up with a thick jute string. But when the butcher handed him the fresh-killed bird, the plastic bag around it worried him. The *vidente* had been very clear: Everything was to be placed in a cotton bag before being cast out on the waters. Wouldn't the plastic block the remedial powers of its contents? He decided he would remove it at the last minute.

He had a difficult time, too, finding a bag made entirely of cotton. There were bags with buckles and straps strewn about the house—bags of shiny, impermeable canvas. But none of those seemed right. After going through the options carefully, he decided on a pillowcase. He placed the chicken parts, the fish, and the snapshot in a sturdy basket, covered them with the cloth, and when five-thirty came at last, he headed for Delfines, a beach due west of his house.

It was a cold gray day, the coastline locked in a rolling fog that curled under his clothes and chilled him to the marrow. He found a place to sit on a large stone near the water's edge and waited for the sky to change. The sea was a leaden blue, ridged by angry waves that rushed toward him in a loud white fury. Far away, like fragile dolls, two lovers walked hand in hand.

He felt ridiculous sitting there with his carcasses, the mist spitting in his face, waiting for the sun to sink into the sea. What in the world had become of him? All his life he had been a skeptic, a resolute agnostic, a man who believed more in the order of a well-made camera than in powers and spirits he couldn't observe. But the truth was the seer had made an impression. How could a total stranger in the dark of an abandoned storefront possibly know his mother's name? Or see what he carried in his pocket? And what spectral being had granted Señor Juan the ability to channel the long-ago thoughts of his dead wife?

Indeed, when Bluhm had staggered out of that fusty ante-room into the windy street, he had taken the velvet pouch from his pocket, examined the little glass tube by the bright light of day, and seen that it was exactly what the *vidente* had said it was. The barbaric physicality of it turned his stomach; he dropped it into the nearest garbage can. And yet here he was, countering that voodoo with a ghoulish confection of his own.

When the fog lifted enough to reveal the sun poised on the horizon, he removed the jute string from the waxed-paper par-cel and dropped the fish heads into the pillowcase. Taking the wire twist from the plastic bag, he threw in the tiny chicken heart along with the bird's wrinkled feet and wings. Blood seeped through the white cotton, staining the dark sand. He took the snapshot from the bottom of the basket and felt the urge to rip his young, insolent face into pieces. He tore it into narrow strips, dropping them one by one into the foul concoc-tion. When he was done, he tied the open end of the pillow-case into a knot, took off his shoes, and rolled his trousers to his knees.

He walked to the surf and waded in, feeling the cold water sting his shins, swirl around his calves. The pillowcase was mostly wet now; large pink drops fell from it into the great repository of ocean. He drew back the bag and flung it hard and high toward the orange disk that hovered like ghostly fire on the horizon. The bag ballooned briefly, then splashed onto the water's surface, just beyond the breaking waves. He could see it float for a few seconds in perfect suspension, until a wave swelled and carried it back, washing it up just a few feet away, covered with seaweed. He waded over and pulled it up, then headed out for a second time. Braving the icy waves, he went deeper, until the water was at his thighs. When the surf broke, he rolled the bag into a tight ball and pitched with all his might toward the sun. It landed in the water, bobbed for a few seconds, puffed white, then collapsed and sank. Relieved, he turned back to shore.

But the pillowcase made it to the beach before he did. He saw it skim past like a swift manta ray, until it dropped, limp, onto the sand. He swore under his breath and pushed against the current, making his way to the cursed rag, when he heard someone shouting. A strange apparition raced toward him: a scrawny man in a shirt so wide, it flapped like the wings of a great bird. His hair was bleached yellow by sun, knit by the wind—and it tumbled over his forehead in a mass of grimy curls. He was shouting and waving his arms up and down, trying urgently to communicate something. But between the darkening sky and the mounting wind, Bluhm couldn't understand a word of what was being said. He stood, holding the dripping pillowcase away from him, rooted to the hard, wet sand.

When the man was close enough, Bluhm saw he was old and wrinkled, with cheeks so hollow there couldn't have been more than a few teeth in his head. There was a dark purple pouch under one eye and grizzled hair bristling from his nostrils. He was deep brown and of that indeterminate age that makes it impossible to tell whether a man is fifty or seventy, but it was clear he had been long in the world.

The man pointed to the white bag and Bluhm thought he might now hear a lecture on how beachgoers shouldn't despoil the scenery, but all he heard was "Gi-i-i-mm."

Bluhm didn't know what that could possibly mean, but it was enough to convince him that the intruder meant no harm, had even perhaps come to help. The old man said it again: "Gi-i-i-mm!" He was smiling genially, his eyes mere slits in a leathery face. He pulled on one ear, waiting for Bluhm to respond, but Bluhm only stared, wondering what to say. Suddenly, the man seized the bag from Bluhm's hands and ran toward the open sea, splashing through the tide like a spirited boy. He kept on, holding the bag in midair until he was waist deep, and then swam out, his head growing smaller and smaller against the scarlet sky. When he was beyond the foam of the roiling surf—no more than a toy against the watery magnitude—he released the bag into the ocean. Bluhm watched it float away, a white speck gliding toward the light, shrinking before his eyes, until he could see it no more.

What unseen force, what astral alignment had brought this stranger to his rescue? Bluhm stood on the shore, his mind reaching wildly, trying to rationalize what he'd just seen. There he'd been, a lone man against an unruly ocean, failing to carry out Señor Juan's orders, when, with no reason or warning, a random beachcomber had appeared and sent the cure out to sea. "Believe it," the *vidente* had said. And, despite the fact that Bluhm didn't believe much of anything—despite his skepticism and inexperience in the secret arts—he wondered whether the seer's gifts had extended to this moment. Could it be more than just unexpected grace?

By the time the man had swum back to shore, Bluhm had collected himself. He rolled down his pants, put on his shoes, and went through his pockets searching for money. When his benefactor emerged from the water, shaking himself dry like an old dog, Bluhm hurried forward to apologize for having nothing with which to repay him.

The stranger put one hand in the air and shook his head. "I didn't do it for money, friend," he said. "I saw a lonely soul trying to rid himself of a curse, and the curse kept on swimming back. What else could I do?"

Bluhm was astonished—first, because the man's speech, apart from its thickness, was actually quite intelligible; second, because he seemed to know exactly why Bluhm was there. "How did you know about the curse?" he said.

The man laughed. "I wasn't born yesterday. You'd be surprised how many men and women I see out here, trying to put their lives in order."

It was dark now, and cold. Bluhm's trousers were clinging to his legs. He began to shiver. "You live close by?"

"I live right here on the beach."

Bluhm looked around, but there was no shack, no tent, nothing but sand and rock. "How? Where do you sleep? How do you eat?"

The man pointed to a dilapidated canoe resting on its side against the stone jetty. "I get by. I fish. This sea is a great, good mother."

"Don't you get cold? Don't you have some kind of roof over your head?"

"I used to have a roof long ago. It only brought me misery."

"What happened?"

"My woman ran off with my best friend. And, as unjust as it sounds, my kids grew to hate me for it."

"Hate you? How could they possibly hate you for such a thing?"

"Nobody likes a loser! The moment she was gone, my boys blamed me for everything. They were full-grown, still leeching off their old man. But our business—a little fruit stall in Magdalena—was losing customers. The people began to go down the road and buy mangoes from someone else. Didn't want to eat my bad luck, I guess." He chuckled and shook his head. "So one morning, after a bad night of bickering with one of my greedy sons, I got up and decided to leave that dump. I just walked out. I thought to myself, Why not? Let *them* worry about the unpaid bills, the mold on the walls, the busted water main! It was the best thing I've ever done," he said confidently. "I'm better off here, wandering the sand."

Bluhm was half aghast, half in awe of the man's warped sense of freedom. How many ragged and dispossessed had Bluhm seen wandering the streets of Lima? And what madman among them would have chosen to live on this stretch of coast, far from the crowds, with no hope of aid or charity? A sharp gale rushed in from the sea, fixing the man's shirt to his skin, lifting his hair from his face so that he seemed suddenly peeled and vulnerable.

"Look," Bluhm shouted against the wind. "I don't know who you are. I don't know why you felt compelled to help me. But I'm grateful and I want to offer you a meal, a little money, some clean clothes. If you come to my house at three hundred Avenida Rivera, I promise you these things."

"Well, well," the old man shouted back, gazing at the sky over Bluhm's head, as if he were trying to find words there. "Very kind. Very kind." But when he finally met Bluhm's eyes again, his voice filled with a sudden intensity. "And if you return with another curse, I'll be here, I'll help you carry it, brother."

THE RECEPTIONIST WAS COLD and officious. She lifted her spectacles to get a better look. "No appointment?" she said.

Maria fingered the wool of her coat. "No," she said nervously, then hastened to explain.

"You can't see the dean without an appointment!" the woman snapped, cutting her off. "He's a busy man. You'll have to come some other time."

The only other person in the waiting room was a well-dressed young man, and he peered at her quizzically over the rim of a medical journal. Maria leaned over the woman's desk and said in her most ingratiating voice, "I understand, ma'am, and you're absolutely right: I should have made an appointment. But would you kindly tell Dr. Weiss that Maria Bluhm, his best friend's wife, is here and would like to say hello?"

The woman raised an eyebrow and sniffed, but she jotted down the name and pointed Maria to a seat. Ten minutes later, when a freckle-faced student emerged from the back, her eyes dewy with adulation, the receptionist called Maria's name and waved her through the door.

The dean's office was spacious and richly appointed, with beige leather sofas and glistening brass lamps. A soft terra-cotta carpet ran the full length and width of the room, at the end of which stood an imposing old desk of carved wood, set at an angle. Dean Weiss had stepped away, the woman explained, and would be back shortly. She left Maria to wander his inner sanctum, take in his shelves of leather-bound books; his lavishly framed photographs of anonymous, happy faces; his wall of diplomas and awards.

"My dear Mrs. Bluhm! So when did you and the old boy get married?" a deep voice boomed behind her.

The years had certainly passed since she had last seen him. She found herself looking at a tall man with a full head of silvery hair. In his navy blue suit, crisp striped shirt, and red wool vest, he looked more like a figure from the society page than the administrator of a school. She was momentarily speechless, doubting she had ever laid eyes on him, but she quickly regained composure. "No. Carlos and I are not married. I lied to your receptionist because it was the only way to get your attention. Was it wrong of me?"

"No! Not wrong at all! It's good to see you."

"It's been a long time."

"It has, but I'd know you anywhere. You're as pretty as

ever." He planted a kiss on her cheek and motioned her to take a seat on the long sofa. She perched on a corner and propped her worn purse on her knees.

"So, tell me. To what do I owe this surprise?" he said amiably, taking the chair opposite her.

"I need your help, Dr. Weiss."

He wagged a hand. "No honorifics, please. Call me Oscar. A woman who has lived with my friend for so many years is certainly entitled to call me by my first name."

"Oscar."

"Good."

"I don't want to alarm you in any way, Oscar. There's nothing wrong with Carlos. He's fine. I came to ask an important personal favor. For me."

"And what would that be?"

"I'd like you to take me on as a patient."

He laughed and ran a hand through his thick hair. "You're full of surprises, aren't you?"

"I'm very serious. You are the only doctor who can help me. I'm prepared to pay whatever you charge. Within certain limits, of course."

He seemed embarrassed and amused all at once. "I don't practice psychiatry any more, Maria. I'm the dean of this institution now."

"Yes. I figured that out when I called the number in Carlos's book. But you are still a doctor of the mind, are you not? You can help me see into someone else's head?"

He smiled and shook his head. "Even if I were still practicing, I wouldn't be able to treat you. I'm simply too close to Bluhm. There are rules about that."

She felt a quick tightness in her throat, and her eyes welled swiftly with tears. It was too much—such high anticipation, met now with this.

"I am happy to refer you to someone else, though. There are lots of fine psychiatrists in this city. It doesn't have to be me, you know."

"Yes, it does!" she cried. "None of them knows Carlos as well as you do!"

"A psychiatrist would try to help *you,* Maria. Not him."

She looked up, barely able to see him through her tears. "The only way to help me is to fix things between me and Carlos," she said, feeling something like anger now. "I don't know anything about your medicine, Oscar. I grew up getting free vaccinations from a government truck that came once a year to the slum where I lived. Whenever there was something wrong, we didn't come to offices like these. We took herbs or lit candles or rubbed lucky stones. I'm not like you. I don't know what goes on in psychiatrists' offices. I'm a *chola.* Probably the only one in this building who isn't cleaning your bathrooms or taking out your garbage. When you say that another doctor would help me, I have no idea what that means. All I know is that I need to understand why, after twenty years, the man I live with won't marry me. I'm afraid more than ever now that I may lose him, and if I lose him, I lose my roof, my security, everything. Do you understand? Everything!"

He stroked his upper lip with his forefinger and studied her. She was just shy of beautiful, still filled with an animal magnetism he couldn't ignore. Her mouth was trembling, but she sat a little straighter now, seeing that her words had penetrated something in his courtly veneer. After a short while he said, "You've changed."

"Have I?"

"Well, I can hardly say I ever knew you. I saw you only a few times, mostly in dark bars with impossibly loud music. But that girl was a mere wisp of a thing. All hair. Frankly, in the beginning I never understood what Bluhm saw in you— what you had that was worth throwing over a whole lifetime of marriage, a whole family. But over the years I've come to realize you were more than I reckoned you for."

She smiled weakly and wiped her tears with the backs of her hands.

"So you're worried about the old fellow?" he said.

"I'm worried he wants to get rid of me."

He started to speak but stopped, struggling with something. Suddenly he was up, pushing away his chair. "No," he said finally, with a voice that brooked no argument, "let's get this straight. I can't take you on as a patient. It's out of the question." Her composure was about to dissolve again when he reached over and squeezed her knee. She looked up, startled by that intimate gesture, and saw a gentler expression. "Don't cry. I haven't finished," he said.

He sat back down, drew closer. "You interest me, Maria. You have since the night I came to Bluhm's house and saw you there with him. Remember?"

"I do." She smiled and added coyly, "I remember your bloody nose." She hurried to take the opening. "How do I interest you, Oscar?"

"Curiosity. Sympathy. You make me want to help you, that's all. Help Bluhm. I'd like to hear you out, give you a word of advice if I can."

She raised a hand toward her heart.

"Well, even if I am dean of this school, I could hardly be accused of malpractice if I talk to my pal's wife on an informal basis, could I? We could meet somewhere, away from this office. Have coffee. Chat with each other as friends."

She shot to her feet, ran around the table, and threw her arms around his neck. Thrusting her face into his thick crop of white hair, she squeezed tight, pressing her breasts against his shoulder. He pulled away and laughed.

"That's quite enough," he said. "More than enough, I'd say."

8

Wounds

TERCIO DE MUERTE

BLUHM COULDN'T PUT SEÑOR JUAN'S WORDS OUT of his mind. Maria did not love him. The man had said it categorically, as if it were obvious—as if it had always been so. Bluhm wanted to dismiss it but instead found himself fretting. How was it that everyone knew more about his life than he did? The maid had suspected Maria was up to no good long before he had stumbled on the evidence. A vagrant he'd met by chance had known he was battling a curse. And now a total stranger with an army of wooden saints was telling him that the woman with whom he lived—his lover of twenty years— did not love him. Perhaps never had.

He hadn't expected to pay the seer another visit, but the anxiety was too much for him. Within two days he was back at the *vidente*'s table.

"You said Maria doesn't love me?"

"She needs you. She wants to keep you. She may even *be-lieve* she loves you. But it is not love. No."

"I don't understand. How can that be? Are you telling me she's never loved me in all the years we've been together? Since the beginning?"

"That's what I see."

Bluhm paused to take it in. "What will become of us, then?" he said finally.

"I see you apart, Carlos Bluhm; but then again, you never really have been together, have you?"

It was an answer so cryptic, so thoroughly unsatisfying, and—for all Bluhm's ensuing questions—so unexplained that Bluhm went off more puzzled than before. He told his friends about it the following evening, at their next gathering at the Marriott bar.

"Too bad Oscar isn't here to help you with that," Marco said, laughing. "I don't have a clue as to what your bogeyman could possibly mean."

"Where is Oscar, anyway?" Willy asked.

"Who knows? He's such a celebrity now," Marco said, "I guess he doesn't have time for his old pals. He called to say he was busy."

Bluhm stared at the brightly lit ceiling. "She and I have been together in every way a man and woman can possibly be," he said. "Why is that seer saying we never really were?"

A long, uncomfortable silence descended. Springing to fill it, Willy put forward a question he had wanted to ask Bluhm for years. "Are you happier now than you were with Sophie?"

Bluhm's eyes grew wide. "Sophie?"

"I've never said this to you, Bluhm, but it always seemed to me that you and Sophie had a fairly happy marriage. A little peccadillo here and there doesn't mean a marriage isn't strong. I carried on with Carmela for fifteen years, but somehow my marriage survived it. I've always wanted to ask you this: What happened there in the end? How could it be that Sophie didn't love you enough to stick with you? And how could it be that you didn't love her enough to want her back?"

Bluhm searched for something to say. "I don't know, Willy," he said finally. "I don't know how much love had to do with it. We just seemed to fall apart of our own accord."

"Bluhm," Marco said, "what Willy is really asking is: What was going on between you and Sophie *before* things fell apart? In those last few months, before you went off with Maria?"

Bluhm couldn't remember much of anything about that time and said so. There were only the long gray days of fulfilling work quotas, shuttling the boys back and forth from school, paying the bills. Sophie was but a dim part of it. The only brightness he could recall were those snatched moments of joy with Maria.

"Okay," Willy said. "Forget it. I was curious, but I don't want to put you through a mill of bad memories."

That night, when Bluhm got home, he noticed that Maria's room was dark, but light was blazing from the slit under his door. He opened the door carefully, soundlessly, to find her sitting on his bed with her back to him, staring at something in her hand. The bedside radio was on, tuned to the philharmonic, and the music was gentle, familiar—a nocturne for string instruments. He closed the door behind him with a sharp click.

When she turned, her face was calm and resolute, as if she had fully expected him to find her. "There you are," she said.

"Yes."

"Where did you get this?" she said, displaying the shaman's stone in the palm of one hand.

"From a seer."

"What did he say?"

He didn't want to goad her but couldn't help himself—the anger and disgust so strong. "He said that you smeared your blood above my door. That there were objects buried in my garden. That there are foreign substances in my food. Possibly poison."

She rose slowly, clenching the talisman in her hand, her lips set in a grim line. But she was silent.

"He called it a curse."

She felt anger well deep within her now. Her eyes began to burn, drawing a fierce heat to her cheeks. It wasn't how she had meant this conversation to go, but he seemed suddenly smug and condescending—the very personification of all she despised about his people. She raised the stone in her fist.

He gave her a bitter smile and snorted. "Funny you should raise your hand against me. Am I not the wronged one here? I can't even eat at my own table."

The arrogance was too much for her. "*My* own table!" she spat back. "*My* door! *My* garden! *My* house! My, my, my! Just listen to yourself."

"I only see things as they are, Maria. Have I said anything that isn't true?"

"You're building a case against me, aren't you? Gathering proof. And now this little stone is your witness."

Bluhm laughed. "You're the one who specializes in witch-craft, remember? I'm just dodging the arrows, trying to figure out what else you've got up your sleeve."

She cast the stone on the bed. It tumbled across the bed-spread, fell to the floor, and bounced toward him. He picked it up. It still held the warmth of her fingers. The sensation was galvanizing, as quick and forceful as an electric charge: She was real, human, a woman he had once loved. He wanted to take her in his arms, feel the heat of her whole body, but she was standing with her fists on her hips, feet firmly apart—just like Carmela. He slipped the stone into his pocket and let the warmth pass from his hand.

"For all my faith in the supernatural, Carlos, that seer is yours, not mine—he can't see through my eyes; he'll never be able to look at the world as I do."

"That simply is not true."

"Oh?" she said.

"He sees through your eyes perfectly. He said you didn't love me. You never have."

Her arms dropped to her sides and her body swayed slightly, as if she'd been punched. But she drew up immedi-ately, the muscles in her jaw tense. "Well," she said, "I guess that man does know a thing or two, doesn't he? I don't love you, Carlos. I don't love you at all."

• • •

"TELL ME A BIT about yourself."

They were in Manolo's, a good distance from the open-air tables where the hard-bitten regulars sat drinking their coffee, hunched against the cold. He stirred sugar into his cortado, watching her hands as they closed nervously around her cup. There was no hesitation in her eyes.

"I was born on the rim of the Amazon jungle," she began steadily. "And we came to Lurigancho when I was three. My father was a skinner in a tiny village on the Ucayali River. He lost everything in a flood, which was why we washed up in this city. He worked as a night attendant in a butcher shop— you know, swabbing the blood from the counters, sweeping the fat and gristle off floors. I remember him walking through our door every morning, smelling of death. That should have told me something, no? He was murdered when I was five. In his own bedroom. With his own knife."

The doctor raised an eyebrow but otherwise betrayed no feeling. "Go on."

"His killer was my mother's lover. She was a laundress for the prison workers of Lurigancho. She died of tuberculosis when I was sixteen. She smoked too much, drank too much, slept with every man who would have her—God!" She paused briefly, then pressed on. "My oldest brother joined the Shining Path at about the time I came to live with Carlos in San Isidro. Life was so crazy back then. We were all too afraid to know any more than we absolutely had to. Last I knew, he was somewhere in the jungle, but he's probably dead now. I haven't heard from him in all these years. My other brother manages to eat by getting jobs here and there, as best he can. I don't see much of him."

"You've managed to tell me about everyone *but* you."

"What did you want to know?"

"About you and Bluhm." The doctor took a long sip of coffee, studying her face all the while.

"I told you. I'm worried he's going to put me out of the house."

"What makes you think that?"

"Remember Carmela? Willy's Carmela?"

"Yes."

"She told me that Carlos is probably seeing another woman. The suspicion alone is driving me crazy. I've used herbs, amulets, rituals to keep him faithful—"

"You believe in that stuff?"

"Yes, I do. I've believed in it all my life. I've *used* it all my life. It won me Carlos in the first place."

"Really? Then why do you need my help?"

"Because he's found a *vidente* of his own."

He dusted the stray sugar from the table. "So he's found someone to read the future and now you want me to do the same for you," he said finally.

She nodded.

"Do me a favor. Put all that voodoo aside for a moment. How do *you* feel about Carlos Bluhm?"

She looked up, startled. "Just yesterday I told him I didn't love him," she said, as if her own words were alien to her. "It's not true! He's the only man I've ever cared about. He taught me how. I didn't know about love until I lived under his roof, learned what it means to feel deeply for a person. I don't think I could feel that for another man."

"Why did you lie to him, then?"

"Because he makes me angry." He could see something like anger sweep over her features now.

Oscar paused and twirled his spoon between his thumb and forefinger. "Look. I'm not a witchman, Maria. I don't do tricks. What I can do—No. What *you* need to do is understand why he makes you angry. Why the anger trumps the love. Ask yourself that and maybe you'll learn a few things about yourself."

She placed her hands on the table and looked at him squarely. "I told you what makes me angry, didn't I? He won't make me his wife!"

"What makes you think he should?"

"I've put in twenty years keeping house for that man, making sure food is on his table, servicing him in bed!"

The doctor didn't hesitate. "Then why do you suppose he's unwilling?"

"I don't know! That's what I want you to tell me!" She was almost shouting, her eyes suddenly wet with tears. Their waiter, who had been chatting amiably with another customer, stopped mid-sentence and gawked. Oscar reached out, patted her hand briskly.

"I'm sorry," she whispered, biting her lower lip, trying to contain herself. "You know," she said finally, "sometimes I can't help but think it's this." She reached out so that one hand hovered between them. "Look at this, Oscar. Look at my skin. This is my problem. He's ashamed."

"But if he were ashamed, why would he have brought you to his house in the first place?"

"Because he knew everyone would take me for his servant! A servant he sleeps with, maybe. But he has always wanted the fancy white people on our street to know he's not stupid enough to make me his wife."

"He's certainly not going to make you his wife if you tell him you don't love him. In the long history of male and female relations all the way back to the Garden, I can't think of one in which a woman's anger ever won over a man."

It was the first thing he'd said that wasn't in the form of a question. She took it away like a hard-won prize.

When she got back to the house, she saw that Flavia had thrown open all the windows. It was a cool, clear autumn day with few clouds in the sky—the sort of day that heralds, if only by contrast, the damp, piercing rawness ahead. Rummaging in her purse for the key, she looked up at the grand old mansion and saw how much of her was in it. There were the rattan sofas she had chosen for the living room, the yellow and blue cushions that echoed the first dress Bluhm had bought her. In the entryway was the spindly table he had ferried home one Saturday from a secondhand shop on Avenida La Paz. She recalled his face when she ran downstairs to look at it—the melancholy cast that said that nothing they could ever buy would equal what had been taken away.

But she had grown to love that house. She had gone from girl to woman under its roof. She had learned something about strength from its iron fence, tenacity from its striving garden, fortitude from its sturdy walls. The house had embraced her in a way no human being could, held her safe from a harsh world outside.

On the veranda she could see the bright white corner of the dollhouse Bluhm had once made for her. He had surprised her with it on her seventeenth birthday, bringing her out in the early-morning haze to see it, laughing at her girlish glee. She had proceeded to spend weeks making cardboard furniture for it, cutting out magazine photographs of a family she imagined inhabiting its rooms. As years went by and the paper curled and the balsa walls grew gray with mold, she tore out the interior structure completely, so that the house stood as a yawning reminder of the vacant hull to which she had come. Bluhm had joked idly about buying a tiny puppy to put in it, but he couldn't muster the resolve to fill yet another emptiness, and so it continued to sit on the veranda, filling instead with regret.

She came in, flung her purse on a chair, and headed for the kitchen to give Flavia instructions for dinner. Tonight she would order up a special meal, apologize to Bluhm for her temper, tell him how much she loved him—how very wrong his *vidente* had been. But as she passed the door to his study, she saw that Flavia was there, on her knees, trying to gather up a mountain of white paper.

"What on earth?" Maria exclaimed.

"It was Señor Bluhm!" the maid whined. "He was looking for something—I don't know what. He seemed so upset. And in such a rush! But he must have found what he wanted, because he stuffed it all into a satchel and ran out the door."

"Where to?"

"I have no idea, señora. He didn't say. But he told me to clean up this pile right away." She laughed bitterly. "He didn't want you to see what a mess he made!"

More likely, Maria thought, he didn't want her to see it at all. She picked up a page and saw that it was some kind of legal document, incomprehensible. What did it mean? What was he up to now? She flung it down and walked briskly from the room.

"Señora," Flavia called out. "What would you like me to make Mr. Bluhm for dinner?"

"Nothing," she snarled. "Yesterday's beans, for all I care!"

"DON'T TELL ME, Bluhm," Marco said, his back to a splendid view of the ocean. "Let me guess. She's going to fight you for the house."

"She has no claim on it," Bluhm said. "No claim whatsoever. I have all the papers to prove it's mine. Right here in this bag. But I've never made a will, and soon I'll be sixty-five. I want to make sure the house goes to my boys. I don't want to die and leave them to sort out a mess they didn't make. Especially if she's on the premises. Do you have a lawyer you could recommend?"

"Of course! But Jesus, Bluhm. All that business about dying! Why don't you just turn her out?"

"I thought of that this morning. It hit me like a slap in the face while I was talking to a customer about a camera. He said he was giving himself a little present for having had the brains to end a relationship with a woman. I thought, Why not? So I asked my boss to give me the rest of the day off. Suddenly things are in focus for me, Marco. Last night she said she doesn't love me. She said it to my face. And then I realized what an idiot I've been all these years. It took a seer to point to the fact that she probably never has loved me . . ."

"Your shaman!"

He nodded. "And so I began to think, what the hell am I doing? Why in hell have I been putting up with this? And now the truth of it is, I'm scared. For the house. For my boys. Can't you see? It's as if I just came out of a coma!"

"It would be the easiest thing in the world to get out of it, Bluhm. Jesus! I'm so thrilled that after all these years you're finally coming to your senses. She's bad news, that woman. As my mother always used to say, 'Slime rises only so high before it starts clinging to walls.' You need to get the police on your side. It's not hard to do. Grease a palm here and there and they'll give her a little scare. A swift kick in the ass. She'll be running out that gate so fast, you'll see nothing but fumes."

Marco ushered Bluhm to a private office on the executive floor of the Marriott and urged him to stay as long as necessary. He stood at the window, watching the winter fog slide over the water. Eventually, he made a call to the lawyer Marco had recommended. His second call was to the plump little woman who kept the appointment book for Señor Juan.

By late afternoon he was sitting on the dilapidated green

couch in the seer's waiting room, half-wondering what madness kept bringing him there, half-filled with anticipation for what the man might say. To date, the seer had said nothing, seen nothing that hadn't turned out to be absolutely provable. In fact, he'd been more reliable, Bluhm mused, than a German machine. Contrary to what Bluhm had always believed about crystal-gazers, Señor Juan's information was detailed, reliable, concrete. Even a divination that at first seemed incomprehensible would gain a certain logic over time. Bluhm had come to understand this. Learning to get the right advice from the *vidente* was like mastering a fine camera. You had to play with the dials, make sense of the calibrations. You had to know what questions to ask.

The first question Bluhm posed when he sat down with the seer got to the heart of things quickly: "What do you see as my greatest difficulty right now, señor?"

"Time," the *vidente* said without hesitation, tapping the table with his hands. "It is short, Carlos Bluhm. Running out."

"I will die soon?"

The seer's eyes fluttered open and one hand moved to his stack of tarot cards, as if the question itself posed danger. "You ask something I cannot answer. Something no *vidente* can tell you. Or, I should say, *will* tell you. What I see is time forced into smaller spaces, the hours constricting. That is your challenge, Mr. Bluhm."

"What about Maria?"

"She sits there. She has all the time in the world."

"You mean she will not leave the house?"

"I see her walking with the ghost of Juan Rulfo. Another

presence in those magnificent rooms." The seer stopped suddenly. "Who is Juan Rulfo?"

"Johann and Rodolfo," Bluhm said. "My grandfather and
father." And suddenly all he could feel was dread; the notion
of that woman in the company of his bigoted forebears sent a
cold shiver up his spine.

"Of course. Johann and Rodolfo Bluhm. The banks. The
parties. The champagne and music under the stars."

"What about my sons, Señor Juan? What about Fritz and
Rudy?"

"They are the children Maria will ultimately give you."

Bluhm was puzzled. He couldn't imagine his sons gaining
anything from a sad and interminable love affair. He stared
through the shadows until he met the *vidente*'s eyes.

"I mean that she is the bridge to your children's love," the
fortune-teller said. "And love is what will ultimately save you."

"Save me?"

"Yes. But time is short. Much will happen quickly."

"And the curse?"

"It was never a curse, exactly. A bit of dark art to keep your
feet tied. The shackle has been removed. The poison dimin-
ished. But the wounds are open and deep."

"One more question, señor, before I go: You told me I love
her. And you said she no longer loves me. Was I wrong not to
make her my wife?"

"That cannot have been wrong, friend. Impossible to be
wrong. If it was truly what was in your heart."

• • •

THE MAN WAS IMPOSING—tall, graceful, with sharp Mediterranean features and a gray suit that signaled a serious profession. Flavia hesitated but let him in. When Maria joined him in the living room, he was immediately solicitous, hurrying forward to shake her hand.

At first she thought he was a camera agent, related in some way to Bluhm's work, but soon it became clear he was an agent of Bluhm himself—a lawyer engaged to resolve questions of property and inheritance. There were words Maria did not comprehend, and she felt, at times, as if he were speaking a foreign language. He droned ahead, and now and then she managed to catch his meaning—how crucial it was, for instance, that people under one roof understand the concept of ownership—but long portions of what he said were so complex and impenetrable that she felt utterly adrift. At last, in total frustration, she put up a desperate hand. "Mr. García," she said, "speak simply, please."

"Of course," he said. He clicked open a sleek brown briefcase and drew out a crisp white envelope. "Here is everything I've said, in more detail and spelled out explicitly. It's a letter addressed to you. You have one week to clear the premises."

But she didn't know what that expression meant. When he left and she opened the letter, she understood only the first line, which established the obvious—that she was a resident of 300 Avenida Nicolás Rivera. She tucked it into her purse and, not knowing what else to do, called Oscar Weiss's office.

• • •

THEY MET AGAIN at Café Manolo's. From the moment she walked in, the doctor could sense her anxiety. As soon as she sat down, she reached into her purse, pulled out the letter, and handed it to him. "I want you to read this. I'm unsure of what it says."

Oscar was visibly uneasy. "I don't think I should read your personal business," he said.

"Why not? You're *hearing* my personal business, aren't you? You're the only one I trust—the only one I'd ask to look at this. Please help me."

He took the envelope, slid out the letter, and then, with more conviction, pulled on his eyeglasses and read. When he finished, his face was a mask of pity.

"What did I tell you?" she said. "It's impossible. I can't understand a word, can you?"

"Yes. I can."

"What does it say?"

"He wants you to leave, Maria. He wants you to take whatever you want from the house and be gone by next Wednesday. You have seven days in that house. Not more."

She blanched, as if he had struck her in the chest. He asked if she wanted water. Or something stronger. As he raised a hand to beckon a waiter, she managed, "No, Oscar. There's no more you can do for me now."

"You're wrong," he said, speaking instinctively as a professional, grasping at what he knew. "Now is when I help, Maria. This is where I go to work."

She did not respond. He saw her mind slip away, retreat to some inner haven. He grabbed her wrist. "I'm no fortune-teller.

I cannot see into your future. For doctors like me, the past is everything. I cannot fix it, but I can help you understand it. That is the gift of my science. That is the value of what I do."

"If it is broken, it is broken," she said with resignation. "What is there to understand?"

That abject capitulation galvanized him further, spurred him with renewed vigor. "You once said you wanted to know what he was thinking. Can we revisit that? Can we go back and address that first request?"

She was silent.

"I won't pretend to know what has gone between you, Maria, but it can't have been easy. You've been together a long time. And Bluhm...well, Bluhm is not plain sailing. We've been friends all our lives, and, even so, he is something of a mystery. On the one hand, a creature of habit. On the other, entirely unpredictable! When he dropped his family for you, for instance. Until it happened, I would have bet my life he wasn't capable of such a thing. It was so sudden. So un-equivocal. So out of character. I thought he would try to save his marriage, but he walked away and never looked back. As if his wife and children never mattered."

"And now he is doing it to me."

"Not so simple. But you are right to think that way. You need to watch for patterns, Maria. You must learn to see things objectively." He paused and shook his head slowly. "You two are very different. Cut from a different cloth."

"Like chicken and goose," she said, her eyes wide and black.

That look of unconditional trust stopped him. He hadn't meant to cross the line, be a psychiatrist to Bluhm's woman.

She took it as simple bafflement. "It's something a fortune-teller once told me. To explain how mismatched we were."

"Like chicken and goose," he repeated. "It's exactly what you are."

SOMEHOW, SHE MADE IT home. She stood at the gate, wondering where she was. Why had she bothered to come back? She owned nothing. Was nothing. She was a throwaway woman. It was as simple as that.

She went to her room and sat on the edge of her bed, seeing little, hearing less, the realities of the world receding, until she was marooned on a corner of box spring. She felt no anger. There was only loneliness, a long, blank future, and sorrow that rode her like a heavy stone.

She thought of her family's shack in the dusty hills of Lurigancho: her father bursting in, the morning sun on his face, the smell of blood and night on his hands. She could hardly picture his features, so young had she been when fate had taken him from her. All she could summon was that last, ruinous day when he had come in the door, one ear cocked to the sounds from his bedroom. And then the rest happened so quickly: the reach for the knife, the screams, the scuffle, and that life-wrenching gasp before the silence. As small as she was, she knew when the other man staggered out, skin glistening with sweat, that her father was no longer among the living.

The only other man she had ever seen naked and oblivious was Bluhm himself. She remembered watching as he waded toward shore—a lone swimmer against the vast ink of sea—his pale skin catching the starlight. She had been a child then, in love with love, thrilled by the prospect of what that visit to the beach might bring her. Standing there in the cover of night, holding the towel she had warmed for him in the little oven, she watched him run his fingers through his wet hair, raise his eyes, and search the glittering sky above.

Had his wife loved him as much as that? Had she, too, stolen to some corner of this house to watch him in his nakedness, peeled to his essential self—a creature of God, loose in the world, alone? She tried to imagine the woman. She'd never even seen a photograph. Judging by the complexion of Bluhm's children, she was fair. More than that, Maria could not envision. Was she tall? Did he choose her clothes? Had he taught her all she knew? She tried to picture a pretty blonde waiting on his mother, shushing the children, thrusting her hips at him on their bed. Maria clutched her head, feeling her mind lurch from wife to children to lawyer, and then the letter, banishing her to oblivion, telling her to go.

She stood slowly, moving her hands mechanically, shedding her dress, her shoes, her underclothes, until she was nude before the mirror. It seemed right to see her body stripped of Bluhm's philanthropies. She didn't know how long she stayed there, studying that nakedness, free of his worldly possessions.

She left the room, went downstairs. It was remarkably easy. She threw open the front door and stepped into the cool of late afternoon, her skin alive to a brisk east wind. She stopped and savored the sensation. But only briefly. She walked on, heading toward the gate. Two cars went by. The passengers didn't seem to notice. She unbolted the gate and stepped into the street. Her life with him had begun on sand, was built on sand. She wanted to feel sand underfoot now.

As she walked down the street toward the sea, she felt unreal, disembodied, as if she were little more than a passing phantom. It seemed right that no one had noticed—that no one cared. She saw one or two women drift by, averting their eyes. As she continued down Dellepiani and crossed Avenida Ejercito, the streets became busier. Some passersby stared and pointed, others laughed as if she were a joke, but no one apprehended her. They let her pass. Nearing the ribbon of road that coiled along the sea cliff, she heard someone say, "I bet she's from the Amazon. You know. From one of those jungle tribes," and then she understood that she was being allowed to walk these streets because here, in this godforsaken capital, she was invisible. It didn't matter whether she got drunk, went naked, begged like a dog along the roadside—she was an indigenous person. They would let her be.

At the edge of the cliff she found a sinuous path that led down the escarpment toward the sea. She scrambled down at a terrifying angle and more than once stumbled on rocks, fell, skinned her knees. But she persisted, her eyes on the reddening sun, lowering swiftly now toward the horizon. She could see the waves pounding the shore with unrelieved fury, calling her name with a frantic rhythm. *Mar-ee-ah!*

Mar-ee-ah! At the foot of the cliff, she bolted across the highway, and then she was there, making her way across the black sand.

She felt no cold, no wind. The water was very close now, and, at last, when she waded in, she was surprised by its warm welcome. The Pacific, as she remembered it, had always been cold and bracing. This was altogether different: as comfortable and accommodating as a womb. She felt it rise along her thighs, lick her sex, embrace her waist. Now there was no floor beneath her, only a fluid space. She pushed her arms and feet against it, paddling ahead. The waves slapped her down, then lifted her up, carrying her toward sunset—carmine red over a glowing sea. At last she was there, where she was meant to be. She ceased moving and yielded to the water. It slipped voluptuously into her hair, covered her face, until she was suspended in an aqueous cradle, drifting and swaying in the vastness. Gray, gray—it was all she saw now. She felt a strange peace descend as the liquid invaded her mouth, her nostrils.

Suddenly she felt a sharp tug, as if a predator had taken hold. The motion was strong, unforgiving—the mandible of a great beast, clamped firmly around her hair. All she could do was flail and thrash until she broke the water's surface, gagging and coughing, spraying the air with brine. Her chest convulsed, fighting against the airlessness. But quite apart from the sound of her own lungs, she heard a rhythmic hacking— a series of high, strident cachinnations. When she spun around to look, she saw it was an old man, bobbing in the water beside her, laughing with unreserved glee.

• • •

Bluhm was in his study, trying to convince himself he was doing the right thing, feeling a wretched loneliness steal over him, when he heard a loud scream from the street, followed by the sounds of two people in voluble, angry argument. They seemed to be no more than fifteen yards away. And then came the buzzer.

He opened the front door and peered into early evening. It was past eight and the neighboring houses were brightly lit, illuminating a gallery of curious faces. He could make out two small figures beyond the gate, under the streetlamp. A woman was flailing her hands and shouting. A man was pulling at her arm, imploring her to calm down. Bluhm stepped into the autumn night, wondering what shreds of miserable humanity had blown his way. But when he came closer, he saw it was the old man who had sent his cure out to sea and, beside him, Maria, her wet hair spiked in a wild crop of horns. Both were barefoot, both wearing enormous, faded shirts that hung in tatters to their knees.

Bluhm opened the gate and Maria immediately pushed past him and into the house. The old man's jaw dropped. "You know her?" he said.

"She lives here," Bluhm answered, despite his own astonishment.

"I'll be damned," the leathery face murmured. "I remembered your promise of clean clothes and warm food. When I saw that unfortunate creature floating out there half dead, I decided to take you up on it for her sake. And you say she lives here! Sainted Jesus. I'll be damned."

Flavia gave a little gasp when she saw the strange sea creature with knotted hair enter her kitchen, but she did as Bluhm said—served him a plate of rice and steaming lentils and retired to her room for the night. As the man ate, he told Bluhm the story of how he had watched the naked woman stagger across the highway. "I followed her on a hunch!" he added. "She'd be dead as shucked clam if I hadn't."

"I don't know what to say," Bluhm told him, "except thank you." He folded his hands on the table, half in prayer, half in an effort to brace himself against this new predicament. "I always seem to be thanking you, don't I?"

"Is she your servant?"

Bluhm snorted and shook his head. "No, she's my woman. But we haven't been on good terms for a while." He frowned, trying to contain his emotion. "I never imagined she would try to harm herself."

"Happens all the time," the old man said, wiping his lips with a shirtsleeve. "You wouldn't believe how many sad sons of bitches I see down there on the beach, trying to sort out life's sorrows."

He had said something like that before, and Bluhm remembered it. "Maybe she wouldn't have gone through with it," he said hopefully. "Maybe she would have come to her senses."

"Could be...could be. But I wasn't about to take that chance."

"Of course not." Bluhm hung his head, feeling a great pity for her wash over him. He hadn't meant for anything like this to happen. "I always thought she was a fighter," he said after a long while.

"We can't be fighters all the time, can we? I'd like a centavo for every big-balled hero who needs to lick his wounds now and then."

"No. We can't be fighters all the time." Bluhm held his head in his hands. "A fortune-teller told me I would survive this, that all the heartache would be worthwhile."

"Well, I'm no fortune-teller, but I have two good eyes in my head and what I see is a man in a big house in the wealthiest part of the city. I see a woman who loves him so much she tries to drown herself when things aren't right. These are riches, my friend. Riches."

"She doesn't love me. She loves what I have. And, by the way, you told me the last time I saw you that you walked away from the roof over your head. As I recall, you didn't think a house and a woman were anything worth keeping."

"That's true," the old man said. "You have a sharp memory." He was picking his teeth with a long nail. "One man's wealth is another man's burden. I never wanted a woman after my wife ran off. What, all that trouble for a little snatch? Sure, sex can be nice, but I didn't see the sense in it. And a house, too, is nice, but not as nice as sleeping under a black dome of sky, with stars."

"I envy you."

"I don't have anything you can't have too, brother. It's when the desire goes the other way around—when someone wants houses and walls—that this goddamn life becomes difficult. I feel sorry for your wet rat of a woman."

Bluhm offered him a bed for the night, but the old man shook his head and said he couldn't imagine sleeping indoors.

Bluhm gave him two clean shirts and a thick alpaca blanket and then stood at the gate for a long while, watching his bene-factor hobble into the night.

Bluhm was headed inside, worrying about Maria, when he heard the shrill ring of the telephone. It was Oscar, asking whether she was all right. Bluhm was momentarily confused, wondering how in God's name Oscar could have guessed that she had thrown herself into the ocean.

"You there, man?" Oscar said. "Listen. She called and asked to meet with me this afternoon. She was very fragile, Bluhm, after I explained what was in that lawyer's letter."

"Why would she have called *you?*"

"We talk from time to time."

"You've been seeing Maria?"

"Christ, Bluhm. Only a couple of times, at Manolo's, for a goddamn cup of coffee. She's been having a tough time. I don't need to tell you."

"So you're her psychiatrist now?" Bluhm shouted.

"No!" Oscar shouted back. "I just sit and listen. I thought it might help you, Bluhm."

"Fuck that, Weiss. I don't need your help." He felt his anger rise. "You're the one who needs help, hear me? Check yourself into a loony bin, doctor. You're nuts." Bluhm slammed down the phone.

What was that scheming little hellcat up to now, infiltrat-ing his most intimate circle, subverting his closest friends? And how could someone as smart as Oscar get roped into it? He ran up the stairs, his fury mounting. He jerked open her door and there she was, sitting in the very middle of the bed, in all her entitled splendor. She was wrapped in a dark green towel, gazing back at him vacantly.

"You've been seeing Oscar?" he shouted. He strode in and hurled shut the door. The resounding slam brought her to her senses.

She had been gathering her strength, contemplating what had possessed her to think life was over. The rabid face gave her all the impulse she needed. She rose up like a cobra. "So?"

He crossed his arms in an effort to control himself, gather his wits. Every cell in his brain, every muscle in his body told him to rush up and throttle her, but he needed to calm himself, simmer down. He took a deep breath and spoke in the most even voice he could manage. "You read my lawyer's letter, Maria. I want you out as soon as possible. I've reached my limit. Go."

She drew up on her haunches, gathering the towel against her breasts now. "Like hell!" she screamed.

HE'D LOCKED HIS DOOR against her. She knew, because she'd tried the knob. Why? she wanted to ask in a level voice and with all the restraint she could muster. Why do this now, after so many years, after all the accrued time and consideration—after nine consecutive nights of tenderness? Had she pressed too hard? Had she misjudged the limits of his forbearance? Had she broadcast her ambition too plainly? For all their twenty years together, for all her attempts to fathom his inscrutable heart, she had to admit she hardly knew him.

But there was more. He had looked old as he'd backed away from her fury, old as he'd turned and fled her room. It was true Bluhm was older than her father would have been had her father survived the cuckold's knife—ten years older, in fact. Perhaps Bluhm was tired; perhaps she had been too hard on him. She began to feel something like self-reproach.

The locked door renewed her pique. She wanted to bang her fists on it, yell about the injustice—tell him a thing or two about her rights. She pressed her forehead to the wood instead. How long she remained in that position, she couldn't tell. In time, she noticed that the light under the door had gone black.

In the refuge of her bed, she pulled the covers over her head and thought about the coldhearted lawyer, the unequivocal letter, her deadly walk to the sea. The day's events scrolled through her brain again and again, until sleep arrived and granted deliverance.

When morning came, determination came with it—as if her flight to the verge of death had been a hallucination. So bizarre had it been, so out of character, that she was grateful to the miraculous old man who had saved her. By seven she was down in the kitchen, telling Flavia to take the morning off. She would attend to Bluhm's breakfast herself, she said. She prepared his favorite dishes: fried eggs over black beans, sweet plantains in milk, fresh pineapple rings topped with papaya, strong coffee with hot cream and raw sugar. When he came down to the dining room at eight-thirty sharp, as was his custom, she was there by his chair, a dish towel in her hands.

He looked haggard and drawn, as if he hadn't slept all night. His eyes were paler than she'd ever seen them; he'd nicked himself on the chin. She wanted to run into his arms, tell him everything would be all right now, but he started to speak and his words hit like bricks.

"I thought you'd be gone by now."

"I thought I would too. But that was yesterday. Today is another day."

"So. You won't be happy until you've brought down the house, sucked all the air out of me. What do you want from me, anyway? My friends? My money? My life?"

"You think you know so much, Carlos Bluhm. You know nothing about what I feel. Nothing. I've been serving you for twenty years and so you go on treating me like a servant. You refuse to give me the respect I deserve, the place I've earned. All I am to you is a warm body, someone to tend to your little empire. You don't give a damn about what I think! What do you know about me, really?"

"I know what I see, woman. And I see a schemer, a conniver, a shark. Bringing that loathsome woman into my house to plan your dark arts! You think I don't know that all that incense, all the warm oils, all those nights in my bed were Carmela's idea? God knows what you two planted around this house. The whole thing makes me sick."

"You have some history with the dark arts yourself, Carlos."

"In war you learn to use the enemy's weapons."

She tried to keep an even temper. "I made you some breakfast."

"Where's Flavia?"

"I gave her the morning off."

He laughed. "I see. You think I'd trust you with breakfast, Maria? What have you put in it this time?"

"Here!" she said. "Why don't you find out?" She picked up the plate of eggs and beans and flung it across the room at him. It crashed against the wall, splattering black and yellow on the wallpaper, spraying porcelain shards in the air. He threw his hands into the air instinctively, protecting his eyes and head. There was a split second in which they looked at each other, searching features for any semblance of the familiar, and then he started across the room toward her, a scowl twisting his face. She retreated, hands in midair, afraid he would strike her now. But he seized her by the wrists, jerking them up toward the ceiling so that her whole body jumped.

"Don't you dare," he growled. "Don't you dare raise your hands against me." His voice was deep, cruel, unrecognizable. She backed away, struggling against his grip.

"Let go of me."

"You want me to let go? There!" he said, and threw her hands back at her. She staggered, trying to keep her footing. "Go on! Get out, you miserable bitch! Go back to where you once belonged!"

"I belong here as much as you do," she said, her voice quivering. "You get out. *You* go!"

"God help me, but I can't remember what possessed me to let you come into this house in the first place," he said. "What ever made me think this would work? One crazy night! A lapse

of judgment! And now we've festered here for twenty years."
He was snarling, sending his spit into the air, edging close. "I
want you out. How many times do I have to say it?"

She lunged toward the table and grabbed the steel knife
that lay by the fruit. It slipped at first, evading her grip, but
she got a firm hold, swept it around, and jabbed at the air between them. He danced away.

"Don't you come near me, you miserable old fuck!" she
roared. "I know about knives. I've seen one sticking out of my
father's back. I'm not afraid to use this on you!"

He hesitated for only an instant, and then came at her
with a ferocity she hadn't anticipated. She thrashed like a
menaced snake, waving the knife in the air. But he didn't relent. He kept on coming, pushing her back, punching her in
the shoulder, until she was pinned against a chair. He kicked
her in the shin and she fell back on it, throwing a hand out to
support herself, but she continued to brandish her weapon.
All at once, he clutched her wrist and squeezed with such
force that the knife dropped and clattered to the floor. He
wrestled her down until her back arched over the chair, and
then he picked up the knife from where it lay. He brought it to
her throat, put its cold, steel prick against the pulsing vein.
He held it there, his face a gruesome mask of rage. Beads of
sweat trickled down his forehead and dropped one by one
onto her mouth. She could taste the salt. Suddenly he drew
back, flung the knife away. It struck the marble tiles, bounced
twice, and skittered across the floor.

He stumbled toward the door. When he looked back, she

was splayed across the chair, unnaturally still—her little hands limp against the wooden legs. He covered his face, dropped to his knees, and wept.

IT SEEMED STRANGE, incomprehensible to be back in that room with his son.

They had walked through the first floor together, Rudy peering through all the doors, until finally he took a seat in the dining room. Bluhm wondered if he had chosen the chair because it was pulled out or because some sixth sense told him it was the altar to which they had brought their belligerence. From where he sat, the young man could see the wall was marred with a deep gash, stained with a greasy agglomeration of dark and bright matter. He folded his hands and offered a weak smile. "The house doesn't look anything like I remember it, Pa," he said.

"No, I don't imagine it does." Bluhm paused, then rumpled his forehead in an effort to remember. "How long has it been since you were last here?"

"Twenty years, four months and a day."

Bluhm's eyebrow rose. "You keep a running count?"

Rudy laughed. "No. I was just thinking about it on my way over. Mother didn't allow us to come here, as you well know. It was strictly verboten. But I can't imagine why, after she died and after all these years, Fritz and I carried on with all those rules."

"Out of respect for her memory."

"Of course."

Bluhm pulled out another chair and sat down. "So, Rudy? Do you want this house?"

Rudy shook his head. His hair was the same tawny mane he'd had as a boy, but now it was brushed back, held in place by pomade, tidy as a billboard idol's. He leaned in and put a hand on his father's shoulder. "No, Pa. I can't use it. Veronica and I have a fine house in Monterrico. You should come out and see it sometime. It has a swimming pool, a big garden, five bedrooms. We're very happy there. And besides," he said, sitting back now, "this place holds too many memories. I couldn't live here now."

"That's what your brother said. He called a little while ago to say he was tied up, couldn't make it. But we had a long and very pleasant conversation. I asked him the same question."

"You should keep it, Pa. Hold on to it as an investment. Even if you sell it in a few years and decide to move in with us."

"Move in with you?"

"Why not? We have a big enough place. Your mother lived with us when we were growing up. Why can't you live with your grandchildren as you get older? It would be good for them. Good for you."

Bluhm was silent, looking at his son's hands with their long white fingers. He wondered whether he still played the cello, still played *"Erbarme Dich"* the way he used to—filling the house with the kind of heartbreak a man could love.

"You still have time for the cello, son?"

"Not much. But if you come live with us, I'll take it out and play for you." There was the old sweet boyishness in his eyes. "Of course, I wouldn't want you to come if I knew you were a happy twosome here," Rudy added. "But I see that's not the case."

"No," Bluhm said. "That's not the case."

"What happened, Pa?"

Bluhm cast his eyes up on the ceiling, trying to hold back the tears that came too often now, and too freely. "It just came apart, son."

Rudy nodded and looked down at his knees.

"I loved her," Bluhm said, trying to explain it. "It was crazy, I know, with none of the logic that ruled my life with your mother. Everything with Maria was fated from the beginning to fail. But, Jesus, I loved her. There was something we had that I never had with anyone else, despite our differences, our ages—despite all the toxins that multiplied over the years. And yet I look back and wonder: Who is she? Who was she? What goes on in that head? It's impossible for me to fathom. Maybe it would have been easier if we'd had friends in common: Mine never liked her. And hers—I suppose—were off in that hellhole in the hills or in some bar. I never met any friend of hers I didn't introduce her to. We never had anyone but each other. We've become like two vines in a hothouse, growing thicker and meaner—bound to strangle each other for air. There are times I worry we'll end by killing each other." He paused there, and then added, "She stopped loving me at some point. I don't know when."

"And when did you stop loving her?"

It was precisely the question Bluhm had been asking himself for weeks. But it felt suddenly wrong to be talking to his son so intimately about an affair that had shattered his mother—that, in the course of a few summer days, had altered the boy's life forever. "I don't know. Sometimes I look at her and feel the old tenderness. Sometimes I turn around and don't recognize her at all. As if she were any stranger. As if she'd just wandered in off the street."

"Where is she now?"

"Upstairs, packing."

"Where will she go?"

"To her brother. To goddamn Carmela. I don't know."

Rudy sighed. "How can I help you, Pa? How can I make this easier?"

Bluhm's eyes filled with tears. Who knew what troubles, what dark, tortured nights of the soul this boy had lived through without him? Rudy had grown into manhood, started a career, fallen in love, gotten married, had children, suffered the deaths of his mother and grandmother—and where had Bluhm been? What selfishness of the moment had consumed him? What had he ever offered his sons except trite words and awkward gestures? And now here was Rudy, wanting to help piece together his broken heart. He put out his hand. Rudy took it, clasped him around the wrist, and the motion had the effect of bringing them up out of their chairs. They rose and embraced.

"I love you, Pa."

The tears were spilling freely now. "I love you too, Rudy," he said, clinging to the young man's strong frame. "I've always loved you, boy. With all my heart."

. . .

SHE SLIPPED INTO BLUHM'S ROOM, where the telephone was. Standing at his window, she had watched him admit a tall, fair-haired man whose face she couldn't quite place. They were probably downstairs, talking now. It was a chance for her to make the call. She dialed nervously, spoke to the haughty woman at the front desk, and then waited for what seemed an interminable time. Finally a man's voice came on the line. "Maria?"

"I'm leaving the house, Oscar."

"When?"

"Now. Soon. This afternoon."

There was a long pause before he spoke again. "You have someplace to go?"

"No," she said. "Carmela is off somewhere. She didn't leave word."

"Willy's woman?"

"Willy's debris."

He paused. "I'm sorry I couldn't help you, Maria. It seems Bluhm's mind is made up."

"I might have killed him this morning." Her voice was trembling. "I had a knife in my hand."

"Jesus."

"But he turned it on me. It was exactly what happened to my father. I wish he'd had the courage to shove it in."

"Are you all right?"

"Yes." But self-pity was filling her voice now. The sound of it made her cry.

"Maybe it's for the best, Maria. You are a strong woman. You're young. You'll find a way."

She was sobbing now. "I know it will never be the same. I know we can never go back. But what did I do that was so wrong, Oscar? Answer me that, will you? Not as a friend, but as a doctor."

"I can't answer that. No one can know what happens between two hearts. Mine is an imperfect science."

"What is it you people do, then?" she shouted.

Oscar waited a long time before he answered. "We teach people to listen."

"That's it? That's all you do?"

"There is no herb that can make two people love each other. Love is a gift. It can't be forced. The best a psychiatrist can do is open a window. Carve a hole in a wall. Sometimes that is enough. Please listen to me: A failure in love is not a failure by either side. Don't blame yourself. Don't blame him." He held back, and then added, "I'd like to see you again, Maria."

She thought about that. "I don't think so, Oscar. No."

BLUHM WATCHED RUDY's sleek blue car glide soundlessly around the corner. He closed the gate, thrust a hand into a pocket, and found the seer's stone, its small, round hardness familiar. He had been transferring it from trouser to trouser for days. He drew it out, studied it in the light. What good was this petrified clod of dirt, after all? Suddenly it seemed silly, the fetish of an old fool. He wanted to hurl it to the dust where it belonged, but he slipped it into his shirt pocket instead, closer to his heart.

"He's coming in now, Oscar. I'd better go." She was still by the window, watching Bluhm linger before he came inside.

"You need help?"

"Not any that you can give me."

"It isn't easy, Maria. Love is never easy. You faced it honorably. You gave it what you could."

"I don't know what you mean, Oscar. You say such incomprehensible things. All I've ever known in life, I learned on a dance floor. It takes work to move with a man. You watch his feet, you hear the music; you give it everything you've got. If he doesn't do the same, the dance is over. You can't fix a lack of feeling. You can only walk away."

Bluhm let Flavia know that he was going out briefly. It was four in the afternoon, there was a rare, full sun in the autumn sky, and suddenly he had an overwhelming urge to be outside, feel the unexpected warmth on his shoulders. He walked along the Avenida Rivera, the brittle leaves of the towering spondia crackling underfoot. He could smell the delicate fragrance of late, stunted fruit on his neighbor's peach trees. Draped over the American diplomat's walls, among the leggy tangle of yellowed growth, was a valiant burst of red bougainvillea. He glanced back at his house—grand, white, aglow in the golden light—and then strolled on, breathing in the neighborhood aromas, headed toward the briny scent of the sea.

There were few pedestrians on the side streets, and once he crossed the roaring traffic on Avenida Ejercito, there were fewer on the Malecón—only two or three boys, clattering by on skateboards. He took a seat on a bench at the vertiginous edge of the cliff, where land surrendered to sea. The water, he saw, was rough, driving toward shore in a constant ferment. The strip of beach between ocean and highway was nearly free of human life—only two souls had ventured out, and they stood well away from the water, sleeves fluttering in the wind.

All at once he saw the small form of the old man. He was perched on a massive boulder, knees drawn up, arms crossed, emperor of a vast tableau. He was facing south, scanning the shore. When he looked unexpectedly toward the ridge, Bluhm sprang to his feet and waved his arms—up, down, up, down— as if Bluhm were a castaway, waiting for salvation. But the old man continued to sit, immobile, his glorious halo of tangled hair bright in the lambent sun. Bluhm lowered his arms, realizing the foolishness of it. How could anyone—much less an old man with weak eyes—recognize him from so great a distance?

He sat on the bench, resigned now to reveries. Once Maria was gone, he hoped for some kind of peace. He had prepared himself for it. And yet what was it the *vidente* had said? That a day would come when Maria would give him his own sons? And so it had been. On the very day of her departure, in a telephone conversation with Fritz, in the visit from Rudy, he had felt a love the likes of which he had never known—strong, instinctive, unequivocal, surprising in its force. He had offered his boys the house, the only thing he owned. And, though neither had any use for it, they'd shown him in the clearest terms that it was he, their father, they wanted. In spite of all that had gone before.

He shifted his eyes back to the old man in the distance. What tragic turn, what imp of want had brought that soul to such a brink, living alone under a boundless sky?

The surf, the sky, the great winged clouds brought Bluhm, all at once, to a memory of the beach in Paracas. It had been late at night and a profusion of stars beamed down, animating the silvery shore. A ragged stand of trees glowed in the distance. He had gone for a quick nude swim and, when he emerged, he had felt new, invigorated. But looking up at the vaulted sky, he was struck by the starry night and its magnitude. It was immense, dwarfing the land and sea. Who was he, after all? A man of no consequence, a speck in a yawning universe. What had he done, what had he ever been that amounted to anything? He stood for a long time, feeling the chill sea air. And then he saw the girl running toward him— eyes lit, her hair a black stream behind—clutching a warm towel in her hands.

He watched the old man rise and walk along the water's edge. A flock of gulls pounded the air, soaring toward the sun. He seemed so content with the loneliness, the helplessness, that feeling of insignificance in the face of a vast sea, vast sky.

"I don't have anything you can't have too, brother," he'd said. And yet he had nothing at all.

Bluhm rose to his feet, pulled there by memory. "We can't be fighters all the time," the old man had also said. Bluhm threshed those words, mixing them freely with the runic declarations of his *vidente*. What was it the seer had told him? That time was short? That he would have to hurry? Bluhm turned and walked quickly from the bluff, putting the bench behind him. And yet, he thought, there was something else . . . something more. By the time he reached Avenida Ejercito, he was at a run, his heart pounding.

When he turned the corner onto Rivera, he saw an enormous car—like an ominous crow—sitting in front of his house. It was Oscar's black Mercedes. Three men sat inside.

Marco was the first to emerge. He faced Bluhm, opening the great gray wings of his arms. Oscar was next, straightening a crisp blue tie. Willy was last, and he exited slowly, his cheerless face telling a whole tale. Bluhm was racing now, gasping for air, the little stone striking his chest. "What?" he shouted. "What!"

THERE WAS LITTLE she wanted. There were some relics, plucked from here and there: the silver pendant, a sunbleached conch, the old pink box—ragged and stained—where she still kept a bit of money. That was all.

She was moving purposefully now, putting things right, straightening her life for all time. She carried her shoes into his room and set them out on the floor, in an orderly little circle. But the sight of them standing there, so sad and worn, made her want to cry. The truth was, she didn't want sympathy. She wanted to leave quickly, make a clean departure. She put the shoes away, stacked all her things in the closet.

When she switched off the lights, his bed almost shone in the dark: neat, white, with its two tidy pillows erect as soldiers. A third lay gutted on its side, the dried lilac spilling onto the night table. The bed seemed to lack all life, as if love had never lived there. As if it had always been the resting place of a tired old man. And yet how well she remembered when it was otherwise. She couldn't help but summon her first night in that room. The night they had nothing but an empty house, a bed, and the new, unreliable world they'd made.

She'd been a girl in the bright prime of life, with a future that held much promise. She recalled how they'd made that bed. He had taken the sheets from the pile his wife had left and together they had smoothed, folded, tucked the hem of the neatly ironed cotton back over the dimpled bedspread. She had watched his hands as they worked—large, strong, with deliberate fingers—and she had wondered, on this eve of their life together, in this bed of his former union, whether those hands would seek her as hungrily as they had the day before.

In bed, the two had stared at the ceiling, awed by the barren house, listening to the roar of cars, watching the lights crawl from one wall to the other. How strange it was, she'd thought, this altered dream-come-true.

She reached toward him, if only to distract him from worry, but he was tense, his arms immobile behind his head.

She skimmed one hand along the white skin of his shoulder. In the dark of night, it glowed like parchment. She felt the warmth of his throat, the plane of his chest, the nipples hardening under her graze. But he didn't move, didn't respond. She let one finger trail down along his belly and, lit by the passing cars, it did a crooked dance as it descended toward his sex.

All of a sudden he grabbed her wrist, his fingers fierce and fast.

"No," he said, his voice unfamiliar. There was no anger there. It was as if he were speaking to someone he hardly knew. "Not now," he said, and the words pushed through the night like a fist, rode the air like regret, then trailed away to silence.

"She's gone," Willy said.

"Where to?" Bluhm asked.

"Who knows?" said Oscar.

"Who cares?" Marco added.

"No!" Bluhm yelled. There was a tight, grim knot in his chest. "When did she go? How?"

"Listen to me," Willy said, circling the car. "We don't know where she is. Your maid just told us she left a little while ago. On foot."

"Come on, then," Bluhm said, spurred by hope now, opening the back door of the car. "We'll find her." The men glanced at one another hesitantly, but they got back in, did as he said.

He made Oscar drive to the main thoroughfare, the Camino Real, scouring the cross streets, looking for a small woman with a large, rolling suitcase. As they turned onto the busy avenue, Bluhm thought to ask, "Why are you all here?"

"I called them," Oscar said. "She told me she was leaving. We figured you needed some company. A stiff drink. A good schnitzel. We didn't figure we'd be chasing after her."

Rush hour had begun, and a throng of pedestrians was making its way up and down the avenue—messengers, vendors, schoolboys, maids—all in a hurry. Once or twice Bluhm spotted a diminutive woman with short copper hair, and his heart leapt before he realized she was a stranger. Why had she left so soon? Why hadn't she waited until he returned? And what route had she taken? His eyes searched the nameless multitude. There were so many people moving in so many directions. He saw her everywhere: in teenage girls with swinging hair, in laughing women with wide-brimmed hats, in dim, nondescript shadows that slipped in and out of view as they sped by, through the darkening afternoon. Twenty years might have granted him an intimate familiarity with the way she held her head, the way she walked, the way she glanced at store windows to see her reflection, but suddenly he could remember nothing. He felt disoriented. Bewildered. What did she look like? What was that shape of face? The precise shade of skin?

"What in the fuck are we doing, Bluhm?" Marco said, jutting his head into the front seat. "You hired a goddamn lawyer to pry that woman out of your life. What more can there be to say?"

"Just one more thing," Bluhm answered, scouring the busy avenue. "And something I need to give her."

"What makes you think you'll find her?" Oscar shot back. "Here, on these streets? In this part of town? You think she'd stick around here?"

Bluhm's eyes widened as if God's grace itself had descended upon them. "Of course not!" he whispered. He grabbed Oscar's arm. "Go toward the city, Weiss! Get on the highway! Now!"

"Don't go nuts on us, Bluhm!" Marco shouted. "What the hell do you want, anyway? What can you possibly give her? A few centavos? A good-bye kiss? Get a grip on yourself, man! You told her to get out. She's gone!"

"No!" Bluhm shouted back. "You don't understand! I was sitting out there on the Malecón, and I suddenly remembered something the *vidente* said. It came all of a sudden, out there by the sea."

"The *vidente*!" Marco exploded. "That fucking quack? You're telling me it's because of *him* that we're here chasing her ass? You're one of us, Bluhm. A man with some education. Not a moron Indian." The car filled with a chorus of recrimination.

Meaning to say something in defense of Maria, Oscar swung the car around the corner, putting a firm foot on the brake. But Bluhm drew himself up, his temper at the breaking point. "Keep going, for Chrissake!" he cried, pounding the dashboard with both fists now. "You call yourselves friends. But, sweet Jesus, if you care about me at all, help me! Go faster! Out to the highway. Toward the center of the city."

Oscar dutifully pointed the car in the direction his agitated friend wanted to go, but his face had lost all color and his voice was full of misgiving. "The center? The fucking, bloody center? How do you propose we find her in that human hell?"

"We won't," Bluhm answered excitedly. "Don't you see? We'll drive through and come out the other side. We'll find her in Lurigancho."

"Bluhm," Willy groaned from the backseat. "Get a grip on yourself!" He was holding his head in his hands. "What are you thinking? You're doing this because of some mumbo jumbo a *vidente* said?"

"It's not mumbo jumbo, Willy. He's the most intelligent man I've ever known. He told me things no ordinary mortal could know. And I should thank you for it. You're the one who sent me to him, remember?"

"So what did this genius tell you?" the psychiatrist asked, his voice full of derision.

Bluhm waved a dismissive hand.

"Carlos, listen to me," Oscar said, his face made bright by the neon billboards on the busy highway. "You're asking me to drive this Mercedes into the worst stinkhole of Lima. You're dragging every one of us into your sad, pathetic mess of an affair. I think we deserve to know what the man said."

Bluhm trained his eyes on the rush of traffic, scanning the jitneys that rumbled alongside. "Okay," he said, as calmly as he could manage. "The *vidente* said he saw Maria walking with Johann and Rodolfo."

"Johann and Rodolfo? Your grandfather and father?" Willy said, in clear disbelief.

"Yes," Bluhm answered. "The very same."

There was a pause as the gray of the urban dust and fumes swirled and they contemplated the seer's vision. "So what does it mean?" Marco said finally.

"Don't you see? My grandfather built the house. My father was born in it. If the *vidente* saw Maria walking with them, it means she was meant to be there. In my house. I'm going to give it to her."

"Give it to her?" "The house?" "Are you insane?" "Jesus!" The men erupted in a volley of shouts, each louder than the last, causing Oscar to veer wildly, so that a din of horns bleated from all sides.

"I knew your father and grandfather, Carlos," said Willy, placing two square hands resolutely on the back of the front seat, "and, frankly, they were men I admired. I don't think either one of them could have imagined you with that woman."

Bluhm could hardly breathe. Everything in his head told him this was not what he needed. What did these men know of her, anyway? What did they know of him? But he didn't have long to ponder it. All at once he caught sight of a jitney that darted from nowhere. "Look!" he yelled, pointing. "It's going to Lurigancho!" The jitney was packed with passengers, loaded with freight, and, in the fading light, Bluhm could see the whole grim lot as they reeled from side to side, bumping against one another, struggling to find purchase. But Maria was not there.

"Listen, pal," Marco spit from the backseat. "I'm not going to sit here while that cunt robs you of everything. Everything

you've got. Everything your ancestors worked for. Didn't you
ask me to help you hire a lawyer to get her the hell out of that
house? Weren't you worried about her making off with your
sons' inheritance?"

"We can't be fighters all the time," Bluhm said, between
his teeth.

"How about your sons?" Willy asked, taken aback. "Aren't
you going to fight for those boys, for Chrissake, Bluhm? What
kind of asshole are you?"

"My boys don't need the house, Willy. Don't want it. They
have places of their own. Rudy wants me to come live with
him now. I think it's time."

His friends fell silent. They gazed at the old man in their
midst. He looked spent, haggard. Age notched his cheeks and
brow. But the eyes were bluer than ever, shining like polished
stones.

"Look," Oscar said, after what seemed an interminable silence. "Over there." His voice was flat, colorless, as if he were
speaking against better instinct.

Bluhm tried to follow his line of vision. But the traffic was
dense, and suddenly there was a profusion of buses lurching
erratically, obscuring one another as they flew to far corners of
the city. "Where? What do you see?"

"Lurigancho," Oscar said, nodding toward the ramshackle
vehicle to their right. "Can you see her? She's in the back,
standing there, behind the tall guy in the brown jacket."

Bluhm craned his neck to see, and indeed there she was,
hurtling into view—a tiny figure in a jittery sea. She was in the

rear of the grimy bus, wearing the blue and yellow dress he had given her decades before, and she looked out of place in it, her matronly bust straining at the bodice. She carried nothing more than a neat white purse and a small plastic bag.

"Don't!" Bluhm bellowed, as they whirled past. Oscar slammed on the brakes, then swung to the right, bringing his sleek black Mercedes behind the rickety vehicle. They could see her clearly now. She seemed serene, contemplative, suspended in a universe of her own.

Bluhm strained forward in his seat, gesturing wildly with his hands. "Maria!" he yelled into the windshield. "Wait!"

They rode then for what seemed an eternity, as night grew black and electric lights overtook the furling city. Maria jostled along, gripping the seat beside her, oblivious to Bluhm's frustration, staring out at the bright windows that lined the Paseo de la República. The traffic was thick and fast now and, as cars darted in front of them, the men grew intent on the chase.

"Keep your nose on her ass!" Marco shouted, when a little blue Honda cut in front of them.

"I'm doing the best I can!" Oscar shouted back, twisting and turning to check lanes on either side.

"How in God's name are you going to tail that heap all the way to Lurigancho?" Willy moaned.

"Watch me," Oscar answered. He was perched forward now, away from his seat, his face the picture of concentration.

"What if it pulls over to let someone out?" Marco barked.

"I'm right behind. It won't matter. When it stops, I stop too," Oscar barked back.

"If only I could get her attention!" Bluhm fretted.

"Forget it," Willy said. "She's never going to see you, Bluhm."

They watched a young man surrender his seat to her. He made his way to the front and leapt from the moving bus to the steps of the Palace of Justice. A succession of red lights followed as the highway slowed and fed into two of the city's main arteries. They stopped and started, stopped and started, watching children do cartwheels in front of the stalled traffic. Or juggle plastic balls. One child approached, her palm up-turned, the whites of her eyes crazed with fever. As she glanced nervously over one shoulder, Bluhm saw the infant on her back, its nose encrusted with mucus.

"I'm locking the doors!" Oscar cried out, and they heard the sharp click of German invulnerability.

"What are we doing, for Chrissake?" Willy whispered. "Don't you know that the deeper we go, the worse it will get?"

Inching on toward the heart of the city, there were more hawkers, standing between lanes, braving the traffic. They were waving candy, boiled corn, ghoulish dolls that dangled from strings. Bluhm could see that Maria's eyes were fixed on that commerce, but her face was expressionless, as if she were hardly there.

"Why don't I get out and bang on her window?" Bluhm wondered out loud.

"And get run over? Or rolled by some thief? You'll do noth-ing of the kind!" Oscar commanded. "You're going to sit right there until she gets off in Lurigancho. We just need to get through this, come out the other side."

The streets of downtown Lima were filled with a sea of people now, pushing, shoving, pressing their wares. As the stately Mercedes crept by, they bent over to peer inside. There were hands trailing along the fenders, fingers brushing the glass. Bluhm's friends stared out like the damned descending the circles of hell, absorbing the misery around them: Blind men festered on pallets. Amputees hobbled on stumps. Mothers cradled sick children.

"She's up!" Bluhm called out. And indeed, when they turned to look, she was on her feet again, elbowing her way to the front of the van. She clutched her purse firmly to her chest and, as she slipped behind her fellow passengers, she was lost momentarily from view.

"She's getting off," Bluhm said.

"How can you be sure?" someone asked.

But there was no time to answer. The jitney took a sharp turn and Oscar trailed close behind. The street was teeming with pedestrians. Loud music blared from stores. A row of makeshift stalls was propped against the walls of a decayed mansion, some selling fried crullers, others, colorful toys. There were dazed monkeys in bamboo cages. Replicas of the saints. A man in a knit cap fed a failing condor, its wings strapped to its chest. "Jesus!" Willy whispered.

Suddenly Maria leapt from the bus. Bluhm saw her right foot touch down and then the little body trip forward until she found her balance. He lunged for the door handle, but Oscar pinned his shoulder. "Don't be stupid!" the doctor shouted, his spittle flying in Bluhm's face.

Bluhm flung open the door with a single motion. Black

asphalt scrolled beneath. He pushed away Oscar's hand and heaved himself from the car, landing badly, stumbling, grabbing at arms, shoulders—anything that could stay him—until he got his footing. Startled faces spun to look, but even as he registered them, he was shoving past. The crowd was so thick he couldn't tell where he was. Was it street or sidewalk? He only knew he had to press ahead, reach her, tell her. He couldn't lose her now.

He lurched on, ramming his way through, keeping his eyes on his receding quarry. She was little more than a half block ahead, moving fast. Taller than anyone in front, he spotted her easily, but there were so many obstacles between them—so much life in the way. He opened his mouth to call, but the only sound he could summon was a hoarse croak. "Mar-r-r!" Then: "Maria!" And louder, "The house! I give you the *house*!"

The people around him were laughing and pointing now. He understood how ridiculous he must seem, a clumsy, red-faced man in obvious extremis. He felt their fingers on his pockets, their hands on his swinging arms. But he made no effort to fight them. "Maria!" he called again, and a cluster of thugs took up the chorus. "Maria!" they yelled, and he saw her cock her head like a fearful animal. But she didn't stop, didn't turn to look or listen. She hunched her tiny shoulders and went on.

SHE HADN'T MEANT TO EXIT the van on that busy street, but she'd had an irresistible impulse to get away from the human stench, walk out under a starlit sky. As she hurried along, she stuffed her purse into the plastic bag with the pink lockbox and pressed them to her racing heart. It was just as well she hadn't gone on to Lurigancho. Who would have been there after so many years? She had saved just enough from household expenses to rent a room for a month—surely she would find work in this bustling metropolis, make a new life, start again.

In the jostle and jangle of the street, she thought she heard her name, but the voices that called out were alien, unfamiliar. How many Marias could there be in this fickle world? She closed her eyes, squeezed them shut, willing away phrases that had rung in her head since morning: I want you. I want you out.

It was over, the long dance done. She had given it what she could. She was walking away now.

"Gringo!" an old woman called as Bluhm stumbled past. And suddenly he was out in the street, a gaggle of horns squealing. He pressed on through the hostilities, unwilling to stop. He could see the back of her head grow smaller, but it was still there: the unmistakable hair, shorn and brassy, glinting in the fluorescent light. Bluhm heard someone shout—a keen expression of malice, but he couldn't make out the exact words. He lumbered ahead, perspiring profusely, trying to keep his eyes on the flowered dress, the square little shoulders. "Old coot!" somebody yelled. "Who do you think you are?"

He reached the curb but didn't know it, and the instant his toe met cement, he was falling forward. One knee hit next, the pain fleet and hot as a devil's hoof. There was a sting as his hands slapped the sidewalk, jerked out—palms flat—scraping the skin raw. He heard the quick, sudden rip of fabric, and then a fierce spasm traveled his leg.

He stood anyway, against all the hurt, determined to keep her in view. But he couldn't see her anymore, couldn't resurrect the smallest part of her. He limped ahead, shouting her name in vain.

How would he find her now? Say what he'd come to say? She had disappeared into the great, vast city, without so much as a backward glance.

She was gone.

That simple truth stopped him. Bluhm looked around. People were tittering, tugging at one another's sleeves.

He was exhausted. His heart rattled like a pent-up bird. He wanted to fly away, go home now—rest under a black dome, with stars. He took a deep breath and the fragrance of apples filled his senses, traveled the deep recesses of his soul.

He could hear familiar voices shouting, "Bluhm! Bluhm!" close behind him.

And then the scent of her trailed to nothing. He stood alone in that whirling multitude, unable to sense anything at all.

Marie Arana was born in Lima, Peru, the daughter of a Peruvian father and a North American mother. She moved to the United States at the age of nine. She graduated from Northwestern University with a degree in Russian language and literature and went on to study Mandarin at Yale-in-China Language Institute and Linguistics at the University of Hong Kong. She is the author of a memoir, *American Chica: Two Worlds, One Childhood*, which was a finalist for the National Book Award; a novel, *Cellophane*, which was a finalist for the John Sargent Sr. First Novel Prize; and the editor of a collection of columns from her *Washington Post* series, *The Writing Life: Writers on How They Think and Work*. She lives with her husband, Jonathan Yardley, in Washington D.C., and Lima, Peru.